THE CONVERSATIONS AT CURLOW CREEK

David Malouf is internationally recognised as one of Australia's finest writers. His novels include *Johnno*, *An Imaginary Life*, *Harland's Half Acre*, *The Great World*, which won the Commonwealth Writers' Prize and the Prix Femina Etranger in 1991, and *Remembering Babylon*, which was shortlisted for the 1993 Booker Prize and won the inaugural IMPAC Dublin Literary Award in 1996. He has also written five collections of poetry and three opera libretti. He lives in Sidney.

BY DAVID MALOUF

Fiction

Johnno
An Imaginary Life
Fly Away Peter
Child's Play
Harland's Half Acre
Antipodes
The Great World
Remembering Babylon
The Conversations at Curlow Creek

Autobiography

12 Edmonstone Street

Poetry

Bicycle and Other Poems
Neighbours in a Thicket
The Year of the Foxes and Other Poems
First Things Last
Wild Lemons
Selected Poems

Libretto

Baa Baa Black Sheep

David Malouf

THE CONVERSATIONS AT CURLOW CREEK

VINTAGE

Published by Vintage 1997

2 4 6 8 10 9 7 5 3 1

Copyright © David Malouf 1996

First published in Great Britain by
Chatto & Windus Ltd, 1996

Vintage
Random House, 20 Vauxhall Bridge Road, London SW1V 2SA

Random House Australia (Pty) Limited
20 Alfred Street, Milsons Point, Sydney
New South Wales 2061, Australia

Random House New Zealand Limited
18 Poland Road, Glenfield,
Auckland 10, New Zealand

Random House South Africa (Pty) Limited
Endulini, 5A Jubilee Road, Parktown 2193, South Africa

Random House UK Limited Reg. No. 954009

A CIP catalogue record for this book
is available from the British Library

ISBN 0 09 974401 5

Printed and bound in Australia by
Griffin Press, Adelaide

To Peter Straus

1

THE ONLY LIGHT in the hut came from the doorway
behind him. Streaming in off the moon-struck plain, it
cast his shadow across the packed earth floor and at an
angle up the slab wall opposite but revealed nothing more
in the stifling gloom than a stub of candle in the neck of a
bottle and the rim of a wooden slop-bucket. Adair's first
thought was, There is no one here, he has escaped, the
bird is flown. It surprised him, after his two-day ride, and
considering all that depended for him on what the man
might have to tell, that he felt relieved. What is it in us,
what is it in *me*, he thought, that we should be so divided
against ourselves, wanting our life and at the same time
afraid of it? He stepped in under the lintel. Behind him it
was the trooper now whose bulk filled the doorway and
broke its light.

'Get out of the light,' he told him. 'It's as dark as the
tomb in here.' But the trooper hung there and did not move.

There was a strong smell on the place of some previous
animal occupant, sheep or goat. That, and the choking sense
of confinement, as if he had stepped underground, must
have confused his senses or he would surely have been
aware of the man's breathing, and of course the moment he
was – it was rackety, broken with phlegm, or perhaps his
chest was injured – he made the fellow out, an agglomer-
ation of rags with its knees drawn up, in which he distin-
guished, as his eyes adjusted, hands clasped over the knees,

bare feet drawn together, a brow gleaming with sweat, though nothing as yet of the features beneath.

'Let's have a light in here,' he told the trooper.

The head was raised at that. One eye was puffed and closed, the other blinked in puzzlement, and Adair was struck by its pulpiness and light. So alive!

He was here, right enough. Still drawing breath. A hulk of flesh still pouring out fetid warmth. The smell he had mistaken for goat was the stink of sour flesh and dirt, with a reminder of what nature had contributed to the slop-bucket.

Adair eased the satchel off his back.

'Are you deaf?' he demanded of the trooper, a lanky, slouching, thick-headed fellow in undershirt and unlaced boots, who continued to stand with his head dipped under the door-frame and one hand on the latch. 'I thought I asked you to fetch a light.'

At last the fellow stirred himself.

'I'll see what I can dig up.'

No promises: the tone, to Adair's fury, that mixture of grudging deference and surly independence that was typical, he thought, of the kind of riff-raff that had been recruited out here, disaffected veterans like this fellow, stubborn and indolent, with their own reasons for rethinking every order, who would do nothing till you lost your temper with them; raw youths, farmboys and such, who could ride a little, handle a gun, and were full of spark and spunk, but had no notion of rank or discipline. But the better part of his irritation, he knew, was tiredness. He had been riding, with little sleep and no chance to wash or change his clothes, for forty-eight hours and still had the dazzle of the plain in his head, an ache he could not throw off.

'Well then,' he said wearily, 'do it, why don't you?'

He continued to regard the bundle of rags, whose gaze

he found uncomfortably absent. It was as if one sort of life had already been extinguished in him and the rude health of the other, which continued, was a mockery of both. The body, all that poundage of flesh and bone, however bruised it might be, however forfeit to the finalities of the law, was still going about its business of pumping blood, pouring out heat, supplying sap to an organism that knew no law but the one it had been following for what – thirty years? Drawing breath from the air, even in this filthy place, and the nourishment it needed to push all that bulk, moment by moment, into an open future. He reeled a little. It was his own body reminding him that he had not eaten, that it craved rest.

'You can leave that,' he told the trooper, who was fumbling with the latch. He had a horror, suddenly, of the dark. 'Just leave it open a little. And hurry with that light.'

'My name is Adair,' he announced when the trooper had gone. 'They've sent me up to see about tomorrow.'

He did not name the business, but it hung in the close air as something palpable, a shadow for which, ten hours from now, this fellow in the corner would provide the substance, the necessary weight that would take it out of the realm of official decree into choking event, then recorded fact.

The man, dipping one shoulder and pushing sideways, shifted that weight, and the movement, slight as it was, drew from him an intake of breath that seemed deafening in the stillness.

'Where's that damned fellow with the light,' Adair asked himself, and was tempted to go to the door and call. Kelsey, was it? No, Kersey. He felt he could not stand another moment of breathing the man's presence in the dark, the mark he had set on the place with his stench, the noisy snuffling up of the mucus in his nose.

In the profession Adair followed death was a constant possibility, part of the deal you made in submitting your body to the world of action and risk. But for this very reason you never considered it. As if allowing no entry to the thought stopped the sharpened blade from entering as well, turned bullets in the air by a kind of magic, closed all the approaches down which cannon-balls might come screaming and singing. The armour that protected you, the enchanted zone you walked in, depended on your refusal to accept that your death, your actual physical removal from the universe and from your own meaty presence and weight and breath, had either a place on the map or an hour in the sequence that was measurable time. But this man's death was announced. It was certain. It made the stink, the deep-chested rackety breath, an irrelevance, mere physical activity that had not yet caught up with the facts, unless the body, as its brute force and rude health intended, was to go on past dawn tomorrow. But that was to consider only nature. What was in operation here was the law.

'I thought,' the man said, his voice thick with phlegm, or it may have been the pain of a pair of broken ribs, 'that you might be a priest.'

'No,' Adair told him. 'I'm a trooper. Like the others.'

There would be no priest – had he really expected it? Where did he think he was? There were only two priests in the whole god-forsaken colony. 'Have they fed you?' he enquired in his official voice.

The man nodded.

'And water? Have you got water?'

The head indicated a pitcher at his right hand.

'Well then,' Adair said.

All a man might want in a place like this, at the end of a long road going nowhere. Barring a priest.

He had not eaten himself since morning and it was almost

nine. Once again he felt the pinch in his belly. He had drunk an hour ago at a creek – the same one, in fact, that ran below the hut and which touched the air here with its mountain coolness, though he had not known it then.

Riding down the rocky slope towards it, he had heard night birds calling from the line of trees that marked its course, and had registered their difference from the ones he had been hearing by day – a habit of observation that belonged to his military training but had also preceded it, and went on in him even when it could have no use.

He could have lain down then and slept, stretched out on the hard earth and taken advantage of the blessed gift of it, the body's easy capacity for absenting and renewing itself, but this wasn't the place to fall asleep in, to give yourself up, even for a moment, to the moonlight that stretched in every direction to the limitless horizon.

He thought of stories he had been told, old folk-tales, of men who had lain down and fallen asleep under a familiar hedge or on the shady side of a rock, and when they woke discovered that half their lifetime had passed, forty years. You could wake up here, he thought, as he stooped to the cold mountain stream, heard the unfamiliar birds hooting and calling out of the dark, watched his horse lower its hairy lip to rippling moonlight, and find whole centuries had elapsed, and how would you ever know it? Who would there be, when you came back rubbing your eyes and yawning, to recognize you or know your name?

My God, he had thought. What a place! He had never in all his life felt so far from the things that were closest to him, from any object that gave him back the comfortable assurance of being in a world of his own kind, a habitable place crowded with other lives – even the lives of ghosts.

Pure tiredness that had been. But now, again, he felt in his head the long ache of the moonlight out there that made nothing of steady nerves and a trained hand; the cold came right through your boots and into your belly, set its grip on your heart. He had that same sense of desolation here, in the cramped hut, because it was still in his head and all around them, that infinity of cold light. How much easier all this might be, he thought, if there were somewhere close by a stretch of companionable stone wall, a wayside cross, the sign of old enduring faith, with an offering at the base of a twist of honeysuckle or a bunch of lily-of-the-valley, a field, fallow perhaps, with just the straggling remnant, among cornflowers, of a crop raised a season back to feed farm animals or to be brought to the table in the form of warm, newly risen bread, on a plate with a blue Greek-key design on it like their everyday ware at Ellersley... Pure tiredness. A weariness beyond refreshment. He was dreaming on his feet.

'I can leave you,' he offered. 'If you like. Or I can stay. It's as you prefer.'

The man looked puzzled by this formality but did not appear to consider, either way. But he did not ask to be left, and Adair, turning away to the crack of light, shouted, 'Hey there. What happened to that lamp?' Then he dragged his satchel out, set it against the wall, and lowered himself, shoulders to the damp slabs, feet extended. The night air that flowed from the door was chill but clean. He turned his face to it in the hope that its touch would cure his tiredness and breathed.

Time enough to begin when they had some light in here. They had all night.

Outside, under a calm sky, the two younger troopers, who were called Langhurst and Garrety, were alone at the fire,

6

which was settled now to a nest of coals above which heat danced in smokeless waves.

Garrety, his hat over his eyes, lay stretched with his boots to the fire in an attitude of easy indolence that belied the speed with which he could snap his lean body into action.

This easiness, of conscience as well as nerve and muscle, was impressive to his companion, who saw it as an indication – not intended perhaps, but he was sensitive even to unintended suggestions – of his own deficiency; he sat hunched into himself with his knees drawn up, his forearms upon them and his big hands dangling. He was going over things, a habit, he found, he could not break, though it went ill with the life he had chosen and was one cause, he had decided, of that deficiency he was so sensitive to and which he was more and more determined to outface.

They had been together, the little group of them, for just on three months – not quite the earliest recruits to the new force that was to police the colony and keep a watch on the western tribes, but very nearly so. Before Jed Snelling was killed they had been four – the black who was with them, Jonas, did not count.

It was just long enough for them to have got to know one another too well; to have built up a store of watchful suspicions, resentments, sources of silent scorn and mockery, of little jockeyings for position, and alliances and betrayals, that sprang less from the grander enterprise they were engaged in than from such simple housekeeping matters as whose turn it was to hobble the horses or fetch water, how much one fellow had claimed of the evening stew, how often one broke wind and another changed his socks – Kersey wore none – or the frequency with which one of them said 'If you foller me meanings' and another 'Holy Smoke!'

After Jed Snelling was gone things had changed. Kersey had been fond of Jed. They had made a team, a loose one, and he and Garrety, for all the scratchiness between them, another.

'We're a couple of old married men, ain't we, Jed?' Kersey had insisted.

This was an exaggeration. Jed was just nineteen, same as him and Garrety, and had been married four months.

But with Jed gone, Kersey had got panicky, afraid of being left out on his own. He still tried, Langhurst thought, in all sorts of ways, to keep on the right side of them, but it was Garrety he wanted to gang with, and he did it by making little cracks and digs that would set them going at one another. It was easy enough – they had always done so, but in a joking way. It was a game between them. But it seemed to Langhurst that Kersey tried now to give their old rivalry another colour, that was darker and came from his own nature.

He wasn't their superior in rank, but his age, he was near forty, the fact that he had been two months longer in the force, and his bitter cynicism, gave him an advantage – at least Langhurst felt so. Garrety did not. Nothing put him at a disadvantage. Still, they were easier, more comfortable with one another, when Kersey was away.

They were the same age – Garrety by seven months the younger. Langhurst had believed at first that this might work in his favour but was not long in discovering his error. Garrety had been on his own, looking out for himself and finding ways to do a little better than survive, since he was nine years old. He had lived in the streets, sleeping in bins and doorways and in odd corners where a drunken officer or some lone woman had tossed him a bit of sacking to roll up in; picking up a coin or two by doing messages, making himself useful to carters or bricklayers, acting as a look-out for fellows who were setting two dogs on one another in the back yard of a pub. Later, when he had the muscle for it, he had worked as a cedar-getter, then as a breaker of horses. All this he told in a wry, laconic style as if it were the most ordinary thing in the world. His lips were sealed – his soul too, Langhurst thought – on the worst things that had happened to him. They took place in the pauses between what he told, where only he saw them, and his slow, half-humorous style concealed it.

He was very easy with himself. Had the nature, Langhurst decided, of a clean, quick animal, darting in and out of situations, attacking with a swift ferocity, then, agile and unscathed, slipping swiftly away, with no indication that it had cost him anything either in thought or sweat.

This was a source of continual wonder to Langhurst, who felt he sweated over everything, either before or – which seemed even more shameful – after, and was at every moment self-consciously aware of the heaviness of his bones, the blood in his neck, in his puffy hands, in his cock. He also felt the pressure in him of words, of the need to get out into the open the feelings he was perplexed by or the thoughts he had been going over and needed to find words for if he was to get them clear.

Garrety appeared to have no such need. You had practically to take him by the neck and shake to get a dozen words out of him, and when they came they were mostly ironical, some humorous comment you had to work at to see the meaning of. What Langhurst missed, he found, was the tumble of competing voices round the table at home, where he had a sister and three younger brothers, all of whom had something to tell. He was impressed but intimidated by the presence in Garrety of so much unexpressed experience.

Experience, he thought. Is that the difference between us? Is that what I lack?

When he looked around at the world he found, though

he tried to hide it, that practically everything was a puzzle to him: women, his own body, the stars, the odd, unexplained noises the country produced out of the dark, the soul, death, perdition. The earlier things, especially women, he thought anyone might be puzzled by, but the others, if conditions had been different, he might have been spared. He felt he had been disadvantaged by being made too aware of them – and then by being offered too little explanation of what they might be.

Garrety acted as if there was nothing in the world that a grown man need be puzzled by.

Of women he had no opinion at all except that it was a grand thing, any chance you got, to fuck them. Perdition he had never heard of, except as a weak oath he would have scorned to use. And once, on the subject of the soul, when Langhurst had rather gingerly brought it up, he had claimed he didn't believe that he or any other fellow had one, and thought it useless to speculate.

This was impressive, but Langhurst found he could not so easily turn his back on a question that seemed to him to be vital, and which, when he considered his own case, guaranteed in him the thing that set him apart but at the same time linked him up to all the rest; the part of him, uncomfortable as it might be on occasion, that was alert and attentive, observing itself and worrying away at its own unlikely motives and desires; and was the agency through which he could, as he put it, think things out, turn them over as he was doing now.

Garrety thought him soft, he knew that, with the milk still on his lip. This was because he had always slept in a bed – though a shared one – and had some schooling. But his parents were poor dairy farmers. He hadn't lived a soft life. He had got up every morning before five, with the ground often white with frost, to linger and warm his feet a moment where one of the cows had been lying, then drive the herd in to be milked, and had been doing this since he was old enough to carry a stick and chuck rocks at the stubborn, bad-tempered cows who would not come at his call. He had calluses to show for the work he did, places where the skin on his hands had broken and festered, leaving scabs. That wasn't the difference between them.

'I was just thinkin',' he said now, breaking into the silence.

Garrety cocked one eye at him from under the hat.

'I was just wonderin' – what *he* must be thinkin'.'

'Who's that?'

'Him. The paddy. I was just wonderin' – you know – what a feller'd have on his mind.'

'What are you worryin' about that for?' Garrety resettled the hat. 'Tain't you, is it?'

'No. It ain't me. A man can wonder, can't 'e?'

'You can. It don't worry me.'

He lay with his hat over his face, his long legs thrust out, enjoying the heat and the restful hour. That was that.

Langhurst frowned and did not settle. This was unsatisfactory. Garrety was a hopeless fellow when it came to conversation. What he had really wanted to go back to was another matter, though it was not unrelated to the present one.

No one when they were recruited had mentioned it. Danger, yes – that was a positive thing – adventure. Though in fact there had been less of both than they had been led to expect, and a lot more of just lying about as they had been doing for the last week, with all the petty quarrels and irritations that wore through any gilded belief they might have had in the heroic.

Then two weeks ago something outrageous had occurred. Something had happened. To Jed Snelling. And in a way that was not just unexpected but utterly uncalled for. Crazy, useless! One minute he was there, part of their nagging quarrels and complaints against one another, and the next he wasn't. Yet everything up to the very moment had been so ordinary. Breakfast as usual, last evening's leftover stew. Socks laid out to dry on a convenient bush. Jed Snelling complaining as usual that he was constipated. The blacks' camp when they came upon it filthy enough but in no way remarkable, the argument, when it started, like a dozen others they had had along the way, with the same lot of difficult old men or surly young ones. But suddenly the shouting had got serious, things were out of hand, and Jed Snelling had with no warning become something unimaginable, a man with a spear in his neck who was on his knees on the rough ground, gurgling – praying maybe, or shouting for his wife or his mother, only you couldn't tell because the words were indistinguishable from the blood that was gushing out of him in an arc like a fountain, all sparkling in the sunlight but turning dark where it was sucked into the droughty earth.

That is what he wanted to talk about.

People were running in all directions, women and children mostly, scattering through the trees.

It was Garrety who took charge. He ran to Jed Snelling, and with his knee in the middle of his back, and one arm around his neck, began to pull out the spear. It was of light wood, sharpened but with no barb, and came out easily enough, with a sucking sound, and Langhurst, who was looking right into Jed Snelling's eyes, had seen his soul come out with it.

That's what he wanted to talk about.

Jed Snelling had slumped in Garrety's arms, gone empty, his head lolling sideways, his face suddenly as pale as potatoes. He was no longer there. Clean gone, just like that!

He wasn't nineteen years old any more, he was no age at all. He wasn't a married man. He didn't have thumbs he could bend right back into his palm – a sign of generosity, they say – or a laugh that at the last minute caught in his throat, where the spear had just been, as if he had swallowed a wishbone.

Later they gathered his few possessions, a penknife, letters, an engraved ring and such, and wrapped them in a big spotted handkerchief, and sent them to his wife, Janet. But Jed Snelling's most intimate possession, Langhurst felt, though neither of them could have intended it, had been passed on to him. It was what he had seen when he had looked into Jed's eyes and right through to where his whole life was gathered up into a single knot, which, with the most tremendous effort, while Garrety applied all his force on one side and Jed Snelling himself on the other, was wrenched right out of him in an agonizing release of which the sucking sound, Langhurst felt, was only the most distant echo.

That is what, on more than one occasion since, he had tried to talk about.

He had seen Jed Snelling's soul go out of his body. Seen it. That was fact. And it wasn't just a breath that came out on a last releasing sigh. It was a knot, a thing the size of a fist, that had to be torn out of the flesh with a violence that was terrific, an effort so all-consuming that it seemed superhuman, and which, when you tried to translate it to your own body, was unimaginable. The mere thought of it and Langhurst broke into a sweat.

That was one thing. But there was something else as well.

He had seen a pig killed often enough. Seen the hot little ball of flesh and muscle, its throat cut, rolling from side to side on its short, powerful legs, go thundering down the length of a paddock till the blood was drained and it toppled. But what struck him now, in Jed Snelling's case, but also his own, was the terrible pressure it must exert all over the surface of the body to come out with such a rush. In your wrists, your throat, your belly. And the terrible energy with which, as he had seen even in so quiet a fellow as Jed Snelling, the heart, like a live thing you could hold in your hands, wet and fat and kicking, had so forcefully jerked it out.

When he was younger he had had a tendency to boils, which came one after the other in crops and which, so his mother said, were an indication of the richness of his blood. Which may have accounted as well for his nosebleeds.

He had grown out of the latter – or almost. Once, when they were just riding along, he had produced one that was prodigious, a real gusher – he might suddenly have been punched in the face by a passing angel. He had had to lie down on the stony ground while the others, still on horseback, looked on. 'Jesus! They told me I was likely to see blood in this game,' Garrety remarked humorously, 'they did warn me of it.' This was before the Jed Snelling business.

Lying there, his head back, swallowing blood, he was glad they did not know of the spoon his mother would have insisted on slipping down his shirt – a domestic detail that might have proved too great a provocation to Garrety's sense of the ridiculous.

The boils were another matter, the plague was not past. The rubbing of the saddle, the sweatiness of his groin, were a constant worry to him. Anxious about every itch or swelling, he spent a good deal of time in private investigation of parts of his body where he knew he was vulnerable, to the point where Garrety, once or twice, had told him if he couldn't stop playing with himself to just take it out, give it a good bashing and be done with it.

'I'm not playin' with myself,' he had insisted hotly, but

14

his blush – once again his blood betrayed him – suggested the opposite.

'Well, stop friggin' about then. It's a bad example to Jonas. An' you're gettin' on my nerves.'

Garrety now shifted his backside, and propping the heel of one boot on the toe of the other, sighted down the long line of his body. 'Anyway,' he said, 'I thought you hated the paddy. I thought you were dead set against 'im.'

'No I'm not.'

'You coulda fooled me. Just a few hours ago you were ready to kill the bastard.'

'No,' he said, looking in the direction of the hut, 'I've got nothin' against 'im. I was mad, that's all. Because 'e jumped me like that. He bloody nearly broke me jaw.'

Garrety laughed. 'He was trying to do you a good turn.' He looked up grinning. 'You'd look a sight better, I reckon, if you didn' have such a pretty jaw.'

This was a stale joke. Langhurst made a face, then turned away and spat.

In their early days together he had made the mistake of confessing to Garrety that he had a twin sister. He was surprised by the effect it had had on the other youth. He was so used to it himself, it had for so long been a settled condition of his existence, that it meant nothing to him. Garrety had stared as if he was some sort of phenomenon – a calf with five feet at a country fair. He had coloured up and said mildly, 'It's nothing. Honest. There's nothing remarkable in it.'

But Garrety was not to be put off.

'You mean she looks like you?'

'Sort of. Well, not exactly – she's a female.' This was meant to be a joke but Garrety for once was too intent to see it. 'She's an old married lady of nineteen.'

The resemblance in fact was closer than he cared to

15

admit. When he was still a skinny, pale-faced kid, his features still small and girlish, it had been a great torment to him – the only one he had ever known. But he had filled out at last, got to be a broad-shouldered, sturdy fellow – the farmwork took care of that. But some notion of his earlier self persisted and he could never be sure that some other fellow, if he got close enough, might not see it.

But Garrety was not just surprised, he was awed.

It did not occur to Langhurst that the other, who had no family at all, might consider this presence not just of a sister but of a twin as yet another example of the way Langhurst, without even being aware of it, was a favoured recipient of the world's unequal gifts.

'I can't imagine it,' he kept saying over and over.

No, Langhurst thought, you wouldn't – and he could see why. It was hard to get your mind around another Garrety, some female version, or even another male one, of his long-boned leatheriness and dark, almost gypsy features, whereas his own broad-faced, crack-lipped blondness was common and repeatable. He had grown up with the plain fact of this continuously before him. If being a twin made him, as Garrety thought, special, it had also brought home to him that he was not.

He sat now with his gorged hands, red with firelight, hanging loose between his knees, and brooded. In his mind he walked back again to the place, just out of the glow of the fire, where the little false move had been made that since this morning had cost him so much silent misery.

He had let the fellow out for a bit of exercise. He had stood at first blinking at the light, and when they walked up and down a little had seemed unsteady on his feet. Langhurst had been regarding him, now that the time was so close, with a kind of curiosity but they did not speak.

He had asked if he could take a piss, and had stood,

docile enough, with his legs apart and his head back, enjoying it, glad maybe to be doing it in the open again. When he stepped back to settle himself in the loose trousers, Langhurst, out of respect for the man's modesty, or perhaps it was his own, had turned away. The next thing he knew he was flying sideways and had the whole weight of the man's body on his chest, fierce breath in his ear, tough arms hurdling his waist. They were struggling in the dirt. In a moment the man's forearm was at his throat. His head was being jerked back so hard he feared his neck would break. Jesus, he had yelled, though no sound came out. He had no breath. Jesus!

He was stronger than he knew or the paddy was weaker. Anyway, he had got himself out of it, he did not know how. They were on their feet again. Blowing air at one another like bulls. But he had the man and knew it. For all his brutal size and strength, the week of being locked up had made him unsteady. He stood wheezing. Filled with a fury that very nearly blinded him – he was outraged that the paddy had taken advantage of him – he had gone in and brought him crashing to the ground and put his boots into the fellow's ribs, into his cheekbone, his groin where he lay curled up in the sand like an enormous baby, using his hands to protect his head.

'For Christ sake,' Garrety had yelled as he and Kersey came running.

The man staggered to his feet. Blood was pouring from his eye. He stood bull-like, the shoulders bunched, head lowered. But before he could do anything Garrety had stepped in as light as ever and delivered him a blow to the jaw, hard and vicious, then stood back with his fists up like a boxer, preparing to go in again if the other showed fight. But he did not. He sank to his knees and his eyes rolled back as if he were about to pass out. Then he recovered, shook his thick head, and looked up at Garrety out of his one good eye in a pitiful, uncomprehending way, as if he could not work out where he had sprung from.

'Here,' Garrety had said, stepping forward to give him a hand.

The man, head lowered, was on all fours. He raised one hand to wave Garrety off, supporting himself, but barely, with the other. He tried to rise, slumped, and Garrety caught him under the arms.

Langhurst, like Kersey, had stood by watching. He had been set aside. It was Garrety who settled the fellow with his back against a tree and stood over him as cool as could be, with scarcely a glow of sweat on his skin. He was a bath of sweat, himself, and still swelling with an outrage he could not contain. His heart hammered, his face burned, his throat felt so thick he could not speak. When the man's eye met his own it was with a look of contempt, but there was fear in it too, of a kind that made him burn with shame. The violence in him, it said, was without rule. When he went to help Garrety get the fellow up, he jerked away from him and would not be touched.

'Yair, well,' he said now, 'I gave him something.'

'I'll say you did. You bloody near killed 'im.'

Garrety said this, he knew, out of kindness, to make him feel good. But he took no pleasure in it.

He thought sometimes that he might act better, have a firmer grip on his own nature, if he had his dog Nellie with him, whom he had brought up from a puppy and owned since he was nine years old, and talked to, and slept with, a companionable warmth against his side, and whose spirit, he believed, was somehow continuous with his own – though he had seen this only when he was riding away and felt for the first time the lack of her close and loyal presence.

'Who's Nellie?' Garrety had asked him once.

'Nellie's my dog. Why?'

''Cos you spent half the night talkin' to 'er. Talk, talk, talk.'

'What did I say?'

He was worried what he might have given away, but the news made him happier than he had felt for a whole month.

'I don't know,' Garrety told him. 'I reckoned it was private. I didn' listen.'

To their left there was a movement at the door of the hut. Kersey appeared. He came back mumbling and began to fuss about among their paraphernalia, getting together the makings of a light.

'I knew 'e'd be like this,' he muttered. 'His reputation has preceded him.'

Garrety laughed.

'What's that?' he said. 'What's his – reputation?'

'Mister bloody punctilious, that's what.'

Garrety laughed again. 'An' what's that when it's at home?'

'A stickler, that's what. You seen the head on 'im. Close cut like that, short an' neat an' regular. That's punctilious.' He tightened his voice in mimicry: ' "I thought I asked for a light." You did. I'm preparin' it, aren't I?' But he deliberately took his time. At last he got the lamp burning, but not before a voice came, calling impatiently from the hut. He went off. A minute later he was back.

'Damn that feller,' he hissed. 'Damn 'im to hell. Damn the both of 'em. I'm sick a' this business. This isn't a man's work.'

The outburst made the two younger men uncomfortable. Kersey had said something like it before. Garrety fixed one eye on the far-off tip of his boot, which was scuffed and broken. Langhurst made a study of his hands. What Kersey said was true but he might have refrained from stating it.

None of them liked the work of this last week or found what they were to do tomorrow acceptable.

Dealing with the blacks was acceptable work. It was what they had signed up for, though they were not proud of what happened when Jed Snelling got killed. They had lost their heads. Two of the blacks were wounded before the party got away. One of them was an old woman who could barely crawl – that wasn't something you could boast about. They had let her drag herself off into the scrub. The other, a big fellow of thirty or so, they had done for with the butts of their muskets. It had seemed at the time to equal things up a bit for Jed Snelling, who was stretched out on the sand with a mass of flies at his throat, and had calmed a little the rage they felt, which was also fear.

It wasn't a good thing but it was the sort of thing that happened. Acceptable. Only for a few days afterwards they had felt low and panicky, too ready to justify to one another an occasion that had exceeded their instructions, which were to make a show, and riding always now with one eye on the horizon and sleeping at night with a look-out, who jumped at the smallest sound, in a world where small sounds, which could not always be identified, were everywhere. Acceptable enough.

So was the tracking down of these rebels as they were called, or bushrangers.

They had come across them in a hollow between two enormous boulders, with giant logs all round that at one time or another had come down in a storm, which made the ground rough and difficult. It was Garrety who had sniffed them out. They sent Jonas back to make contact with another group, who were working the other side of the mountain, and waited under cover for thirty-six hours for them to come up, afraid at every moment of being spotted. But the little group – there were five of them –

20

seemed to believe they were invulnerable, or invisible, out here at the end of nowhere.

They got to know each one of them: Dolan, the tall one, almost a giant, who was the leader, the lumbering paddy, a skinny kid they called Lukey, or Luke, who was always larking about and whose tomfoolery, of which they were forced to be the silent spectators, was unsettling – the gang's reputation for murderous ferocity had not included the possibility of a red-haired jack-in-the-box – but dangerous too. He was everywhere. You never knew where he would turn up next.

From the shaky security of their post above the gully, they watched them wander off, in private, to take a shit. Heard the crack of shots as they hunted game back in the scrub, and the young one, at night, singing songs that were comic or bawdy in a raw kid's voice and the others laughing, but they were too far off to catch the words. They had nothing to eat themselves but some dry biscuit and suffered horribly from heat and thirst. Then when the others crept up, they waited again, all through a long night, and went in only when the mist with the sun behind it came creeping in along the valley, and got three of them before they were on their feet, still groggy with sleep. The carrot-top, Lukey, got away and the paddy was left wounded.

It would have been cleaner all round if he too had done the decent thing and died with his mates, but the bullet he got had bounced off his thick Irish skull and done no more than stun him, and none of them was prepared to shoot him point blank, like a dog. So the others set off after the one who got away – got him too, three days later – and they had put the paddy on the best of the horses and brought him here till it was decided what was to be done with him. No one wanted him in town where he might arouse interest.

The rumour was that those fellers, out there, had been

raising up the blacks to help in some sort of rebellion. Among the Irish – it was always that, the Irish. So they had brought him in here, to Curlow Creek, and with no authority among themselves had had to sit it out till the authorities in Sydney came to a decision. Nine days. While the stench in the hut got worse every hour, and the chance greater of his breaking out, or some body of whites, or blacks even, who were all around, hidden deep in the country, coming in to spring him. All their nerves were on edge. Even more when the news came, a paper signed by the Governor, that he was to be topped, but not till an officer had arrived who would take charge of the business and make it official. In the meantime they were gaolers, but every bit as confined as he was, in a place where they had continually to be on the watch and were always at risk.

They had Jonas to scour the bush for tracks and signs of watchers. He came from the coast, which was presumed to mean that he would have no loyalty to the locals, but who could tell what might go on in the head of a black?

I'll trust to meself, thanks very much, was Garrety's attitude. He went out independently, with Langhurst to back him up. He was as good a tracker as any black. Better, Langhurst thought, he was uncanny. He knew before Jonas did what sort of weather was on the way, could read every sign in the sky, every shift of the air, every movement of the clouds, as if, when he looked up, his black eyes narrowed, his mouth at work on a grass-stalk, there was some intimate connection between the clouds' purpose and his own light but restless spirit. He knew every print in the sand, whether it was scrub-turkey or one of the many kinds of pigeon, or one of the bush-feeders that for some reason had alighted a moment and left the mark of its foot, honey-eater or shrike or wren; or a wallaby, and of what size and weight, or one of the many smaller creatures that lived their own lives back in the brush. He could smell the different sorts of grasses, and tell at a hundred feet where a troop of kangaroo had passed, and how long ago, an hour or last night.

Often he would know a good mile beforehand what they were about to face up ahead, as if he had been there on some previous journey – but it couldn't be that, Langhurst thought. They were always moving into unknown country.

It was as if some shadow of him had detached itself and been sent ahead, while he was still there in the saddle beside them, riding with that easy slouch he had of his long torso, and with that sharp smell of sweat on him that was unmistakable, so that you knew at any time just where he was, to this side or the other of you, or before or behind.

Jonas observed all this and was spooked. It wasn't that he felt intimidated by a rival – rivalry was a thing he could barcly have conceived of – but Garrety's knowledge came from a source he did not care to recognize. He would let nothing that Garrety had prepared pass his lips and touch nothing he had laid a hand on.

'You, gub,' he would tell Langhurst when he had something to impart, though most often it was Garrety who would better have understood. Kersey would raise his eyebrows in silent mockery. Garrety, very pointedly, looked away. And Langhurst, not entirely displeased but making light of it before the others, would incline his head to receive the whispered information.

He did not ask what it might be in him that made him the only one among them Jonas trusted. There was a sense in which, for all the time he spent turning things over as he put it, and examining his own ways and reasons, he remained ignorant of how others saw him. It would have surprised him to hear that there was a quality in him (even Garrety felt it) that appealed to rougher natures and made

23

them softly protective of him, and that he made use of this without knowing it was there. Kersey was always doing little favours for him that he barely noticed, though Garrety did. Garrety, who felt he had received no favours from the world, and expected none, did not begrudge his friend a gift that would always make life easy for him, but he wondered at it; where it came from, why it should be extended to one man and not another, and felt that for Langhurst's own sake he ought not to indulge it.

'So,' Langhurst said now, when it was clear that Kersey was going to go on for the next ten minutes chewing over some injury he felt had been done him, 'what's 'e doin' in there?'

'Who's that? Who are you referrin' to? Him or mister bloody O'Dare?'

'Is that 'is name? O'Dare?'

'That's it.' Kersey sat back on his heel and spat into the fire. 'You tell me, son, an' we'll both know. They're talkin'.'

'What about?'

'The price of eggs. Well, what do you expect? How should I know?'

Garrety laughed. 'You mean you didn' listen?'

'No, I did not. 'Cause I ain't interested. Either in him or the other one neither.'

'Well anyway,' Langhurst said, half to himself, 'he won't be lonely.' He lay back with his arms folded easily under his head.

No, he thought. That's not true. A man'd be lonely anyway. He reached for his blanket, rolled himself tight in it, as in a cocoon, and lay back, but on one arm now, facing the fire.

On the other side of it Jonas sat, still and upright. He had been there all this while, but as if he were not there at all; so still and black that he seemed hardly to breathe. You could have missed him altogether except for the sheen the fire made on his coaly skin. Or to turn it the other way about, Langhurst thought, as if *they* were not there, and he was sitting out here on his own under the big night, with the sounds of nearby night-birds calling out of the open spaces, sudden screeches, screams, that were, each one, like long scratches on the blackness of the night, which only deepened the silence and your sense of being lost in it, in fearful loneliness.

'This is a damned dismal place to die in,' he found himself saying.

'You ain't dyin',' Garrety told him. 'That's not dyin', it's just the pain in the gut you got from Kersey's stew.'

'Ah, that's better,' Adair said, getting to his feet as a flicker of light appeared and Kersey arrived with the lamp. 'Just set it down there. Good, good, that's better, eh? You can shut the door now. Only don't bolt it, just set it to. That's right.'

The hut, no longer dark, immediately developed a different aspect, seemed lived in, habitable. The air too seemed easier to breathe. There were rafters overhead from which cobwebs hung. So there were spiders out here! A broken cot. A shelf that ran the length of one wall, with a clutter of tools and domestic utensils, including a rusty mangle. He settled, and the man, accepting perhaps that they were meant to spend a little time together, set his gaze to study him.

It was the gaze of a man who was past what might have been a lifetime's habit of practised subservience, of lying low and making himself small. It was utterly direct and Adair felt himself stiffen. He was not used to being scrutinized. The impression he gave of being cold, unapproachably grim, meant that few men looked hard at him. It was an impression, he knew, that would do him no service here, might even, since their time was short, work against him. But the man must have seen through his formal mask – was he so acute? – or perhaps, after so long alone, he was hungry for contact, or simply beyond caring, because he said after a moment, politely enough but without unfixing his gaze, 'Can I ask you something, sir?'

'Of course.'

'Luke Cassidy,' he said. He did flinch then with a painful creasing of the flesh around his eyes. 'Did he by any chance get away?'

'No.'

'He's been taken then?'

'No,' he said. 'They baled him up in a barn. There was a fight. He was shot.'

'Killed?'

When Adair's silence confirmed this he lowered his head and said gruffly, 'I see.'

'Can I ask,' he said after a moment, 'where was this, sir?'

Adair named the place, and the man nodded, as if the name gave the brute fact a firmer existence, though it designated nothing more, in strict geographical terms, than a bare-floored shanty pub on what was grandly called the Highway.

Adair had seen the body but did not say so. A skinny, red-headed fellow with his arms crossed on his narrow chest, big feet sticking out of trousers that he had outgrown, big hands folded. Laid out on a plank between two chairs.

All day, in drizzling rain, people had come in from the surrounding farms and brought their children, some of them two-year-olds in their fathers' arms, to stare at a real bushranger, his jaw tied up with a strip of torn shirt, where it had been shot away taking with it most of his teeth: a sight

26

fearsome enough to satisfy the imagination of the most pious shopkeeper or industrious freeholder as to the malignity of outlaws and the wisdom of the authorities in having them hunted down and exterminated.

The man had gone into himself. He sat hunched and silent, and whatever he felt was expressed by a vigorous rubbing of his cropped scalp with the palm of one hand.

'I'm the last, then,' he said, but it was to himself the thought was uttered, and once again he returned to silent musing.

Perhaps he had not thought of himself as the one among them who would be left to tell the tale. Perhaps he felt it was a mark against him, against his courage, his loyalty. He rubbed again at his skull. 'I wouldn't of thought,' he said, 'that ol' Lukey'd get himself killed. It's a shame, that. He was just a kid, you know. Not fifteen.'

He stated this flatly. It did not seem like an accusation. But when he raised his head the one eye had a glint of malice in it, concealed like a blade in a sleeve, and Adair saw that for all the impression he gave of being cowed and innocuous there was a reserve of anger in the man, of settled savagery.

'So,' he said, making a hard line of his broken mouth, 'that's the end of it then,' and might have been, at this moment, with his puffed eyes and hacked skull, and the grime he was streaked with, the very embodiment of that human recalcitrance that for six months had filled the colony with rumours – most of them exaggerated and absurd – of rebellion or uprising and not all of them, Adair thought, as firmly discouraged by the authorities as they might have been.

The man began, rather fussily, on a series of little house-keeping arrangements that had to do with settling his body at a more comfortable angle against the wall and drawing a bit of sacking round his shoulders, but were really, Adair saw, a way of coming to terms with the intelligence he had been given, with the absoluteness now of his own isolation, with whatever he might feel of grief.

'Could I ask you something else?' he said. 'It's just that I thought at first – you know, that you might of been the priest – '

'I'm not.'

'I know that, sir. But you're an educated man, I see that, an' I'm ignorant, I never learned. To read, like. Nothing. There's a lot that happens in the world that a feller like me doesn't never get the bearings of.'

'And you think fellers like me do?'

'Don't you, sir?'

'No.'

'I'm sorry, sir. I just thought, you bein' Irish an' that, you wouldn' mind me askin'.'

'Well, so long as you don't expect me to have an answer. What is it?'

There came then the first of the man's awkward questions, each of which, Adair found, caught him on the raw, since they went straight to the centre of his own thoughts, his own confusions, as if this illiterate fellow had somehow dipped into the dark of his head and drawn up the very questions he had chosen not to find words for.

'It's just, sir, that I've been thinkin'. There must be a reason – an' that, you know, if I don't ask now then I'll never know.'

'For what? A reason for what?'

'For them fellers out there bein' troopers' – his fingers came to the puffy flesh to one side of his eye – 'and Luke Cassidy not. For what happens.'

Adair shook his head. 'Carney,' he said – it was the first time he had used the man's name, and he recognized, as the

28

man did also, that it represented a quickening of the space between them – 'I don't have an answer to that. No one has.'

The man considered this. Then looking up with a gaze Adair found unsettlingly steady: 'You know, sir, there's a lot of injustice in the world.'

A statement ordinary enough, but what he heard behind it, or thought he heard, was the echo of another voice. He felt strongly another, a third presence in the closeness of the hut, and with his heart sounding above the rasping of Daniel Carney's breathing, he asked: 'Did you hear that from him? From Dolan?'

The man seemed surprised.

'No, sir. Well, yes, I might of done. But maybe I thought of it for meself. A man will start askin' questions sooner or later, if he's a man at all. Even an ignorant one. Maybe an Irishman asks 'em sooner than most. You'd understand that, sir, bein' Irish yourself.'

Adair accepted the rebuke. There is more to this fellow, he thought, than I've given him credit for.

'So what did he say?' he persisted. 'About injustice.'

'Dolan?'

'Yes.'

The man's face softened. He sat with his head lowered a moment. 'He said it was why we were fighting. At the end, when things got bad.'

'Only then?'

'Well, before that – you know, we had it all our own way. For a while. We could do what we liked. We went into the towns an' that. Took what we wanted.'

'You killed a man at Harewood.'

'We did, sir, it's true. A man was killed.'

'And at Graceville.'

He shook his head and for a moment the air was filled

29

with a kind of high-pitched keening. Adair was confused. It did not appear to be the man, Daniel Carney, who was making it. 'We had bad luck. Things turned against us. But there's a lot of lies told as well. About what we did.'

'You say you were fighting – what did you say? – for justice? What sort of justice was that?'

'I don't know, sir. We wanted to be free.'

'Did *he* tell you that?'

'Maybe.'

What he hoped for was that the man would open up, pluck back out of that world he was looking into with such wounded intensity some form of words, half a dozen might be enough, in which he would hear clearly, and without a shadow of doubt at last, the timbre of Fergus's voice, whatever name he was hiding behind, whatever character he had assumed; a passion he would recognize immediately, even from the broken mouth of this last of his followers.

'And you believed him?'

The man looked him hard in the face. 'No sir, to be truthful I did not.' The admission appeared to affect him. He became agitated. 'What does it mean, anyway? Free. *He* might have been – and McBride. But not Lonergan. Not me.'

'So if it wasn't freedom, what was it? For you, I mean. What do *you* think?'

The man shook his head again. Stared harder than ever into the gloom before him. 'I thought we were trapped. Like animals. That we had no choice. That we were fighting to stay alive. Not to get caught and be sent back.'

'Did you say that to him?'

'No, sir, I didn't have to, he knew what I was, what it would be in my case, a feller like me. But he knew another thing too. That I was loyal. That I'd stick to him to the death. I don't reckon he expected any more of me, or of any of us.'

'And what did you expect of him?'

The man's brow furrowed. His mouth opened. The tongue was visible for a moment and seemed about to form words, but he must have thought better of what he had to say, or could not find the words to say it. He let his jaw sink into the crook of his arm and sat like that, seeing whatever it was in the darkness that made his eyes moist and endowed him with all the dignity of the most solemn grief.

'That if there was a way out of all that, he'd find it,' he said softly, 'if any man could.'

He looked up suddenly. 'I never knew any man like him, sir, not here, not in Ireland. He stood six feet six in his socks. There was no horse wouldn't come to him, walk right up to where he held his hand out and put its nose in his palm as if he was sweet-talkin' them every step in some language only horses know, and him all the while just standin' there, not sayin' a word – '

'Go on,' Adair found himself saying, and broke the spell. 'How do you mean, sir?'

Go on seeing him, he had meant, and he will be here. He will step right in out of the moonlight and we will both see him. Could there be two such? He did not believe it. Fergus. It must be. To have got so close and missed him, and for this fellow Carney to be the only source of proof!

But the spell was broken.

'I think, if you don't mind, sir,' the man said after a moment, 'I'll just sleep a bit.'

It was, Adair saw, a kind of politeness, a way of saying that he wanted for a time to be alone with his thoughts. 'Good-night, sir.'

Reluctantly Adair let him go. 'Good-night,' he said. He

meant to stay alert. Talk between them, he thought, might pick up again. But when he lay his head back against the wall he began, almost immediately, to drift off.

But Carney was not finished after all.

'Can I just ask, sir, what part of Ireland it is you're from?'

'Ballinahinch,' Adair told him out of half-sleep, 'in the west. Near Oughterard. Not far from Galway.'

'Ah! I've heard of it,' Carney said.

'From one of the others?' Adair asked, fully awake again.

'No, sir, I don't think so. But I might have been there, you know. I think I have, too. On me travels. I done a lot of trampin' at one time. You know, after work. Maybe it was when you was there, sir.'

'Maybe.'

'Them days I tramped all over. This place and that. On the move.'

His voice had a far-off quality, as if he might, in these few phrases, be looking back over a whole life. Adair knew he should keep him talking but his body was already plunging downward and he could do nothing but follow it. He had a flash of the view from the Great Room at the Park as he had first seen it as a child, three long windows each with its framed landscape like three giant pictures, all different – before Virgilia took him by the hand and led him to the low sill of one of them and he understood that it was one stretch of land out there. The lawns of the park, with deer grazing and occasionally freezing, looking up out of their other life as if they could not make out what you might be, the change of scent there in the close distance, a presence not yet embodied, the light on the soft fur of their underbellies an unearthly glow. And beyond, great oaks, the wood Eamon Fitzgibbon had planted in 'seventy-six. Then, further off, the powdery blue of mountains, faint as breath where they faded away into bluish air, the Twelve Pins.

'It's a long way off, eh?' a voice was saying. But it was not so far. Not far at all, Adair thought, his head rolled back against the wall. Close even. So close you could let the breath go from your body and step right back into it, instantly. Instantly. The deer, knowing what it is now that has stepped into their world, scatter, their pale rumps dancing from side to side, hooves kicking back as you approach.

2

It was one of the many contradictions of Adair's existence that though he was by nature a man who would have liked nothing better than to see the sun rise and set each day on the same bit of turf, he had spent all the years of his manhood, thirteen to be precise, in one foreign army or another far from home – if by home one means not four walls and a roof, with a fire and a chair before it, but the place of one's earliest affection, where that handful of men and women may be found who alone in all the world know a little of your wants, your habits, the affairs that come nearest your heart, and who care for them.

He was born in Dublin but had no memory of that place except the odd one of steps going down into a greasy area below a creaking gate, and the smell of cats' piss and coal, of cats' piss *on* coal. Nothing more for the two years he must have spent crawling about the carpets of the various lodging houses his parents lived in, clutching at the edge of a table or a convenient skirt, or the series of old women or slovenly girls in whose charge he was left, and who fed and changed him and lugged him about the room when he cried. Not the snatch of a song one of his parents might have been going over at the piano or the smell of his father's whiskers or his mother's neck.

His parents had been professional opera-singers. When he was not quite three they had been lost with the packet-boat from Holyhead, two of seventy-three souls who were drowned that February night and washed up in the days that followed on various parts of the coast. He had no memory of them and had not inherited their talent. He was not tone-deaf but could barely, even in consort, carry a tune – a fact he had deeply puzzled over. He wondered which of his parents' qualities he *had* inherited, and if none, where his own came from: his doggedness, the sternness of manner that had given him, among his fellow officers, a reputation for being iron-hard and indefatigable but none for good-fellowship or gaiety, and among the ranks for being a devil for the rules.

Those who pretended to know more of him than they did – the wives of his fellow officers, who in the little garrison towns he had served in were the authorities on everyone and everything – gave it out as their settled opinion that he was a spoiled priest. So much for the accident of being Irish and for what one man, one woman, may know of another.

It was true that there was something in his nature that was grave and admired restraint. But restraint did not come naturally to him. What he saw when he looked into himself was laxity, a tendency to dreamy confusion and a pleasure too in giving himself up to it, a dampness of soul for which he had a kind of hopeless scorn and which he feared might after all be part of his operatic inheritance. He had grasped at an early age that few things are as simple as they appear or as we might wish them to be, and people never. He had a high regard for the incomprehensible. Perplexity, he thought, was the most natural consequence of one's being in the world – which did not mean that one should yield to it, or to the disorder which, unless one took a firm hand, was its unhappy consequence. He had a horror of disorder, and when he had a horror of a thing it was usually, he found, because he had discovered it so plainly in himself.

Disorder. Carelessness. He had seen a good deal of both, and believed he had been their victim, though it was not in his nature to complain.

From what he could gather of his parents, they had lived very much like gypsies, carefree and, except in the exercise of their art, entirely without discipline. When he looked back he thought he saw a miserable creature of a year or so sitting tear-stained and fly-tormented in his own mess. The gypsy state had no romance for him but he wondered if it had not, for all that, left its mark. He was torn between an obsessive fastidiousness and a fascination, which belonged to his secret and sensual life, with dirt.

While he was serving in Austria he had become for the first time a frequenter of opera. Even the poorest garrison town had its opera house and resident company, and he had gone back night after night, drawn by the belief that he might catch, behind the tawdry spectacle that saw lovers drive one another to the highest pitch of emotion and left the stage strewn with corpses, some shadow of that couple, his parents, who had once given life to these roles and whose spirit the roles themselves might reflect.

He was surprised how fiercely his own emotions were caught up, how shaken he was. It was not his parents he saw in these savage creatures, in whom a kind of madness, a rage for self-destruction, was made by the music to seem like the highest goal of life, the most exquisite pleasure, but, in a shadowy reflection of their own drama, Virgilia and himself.

His large capacity for irony had no force against the magic of it. He told himself it was a hoax, all elaborate illusionism; that the costumes which appeared so fine had sweat-stains at the armpits and were soiled and worn, that under the greasepaint the singers were sweating like ordinary citizens and were the same dyed-haired, loud-tongued crew who, after the performance, would come tumbling into the dirty little tavern opposite. There they would be hailed with a chorus of shouts, and his drunken fellow-officers would squeeze up, all coarse wool and leather, to make room at the table for these ex-goddesses and slave-girls and nymphs who, if they were to ride on clouds again, would do so, after a litre of mulled wine and a steaming dish of wurst and sauerkraut, on goose-feathers in one of the tavern's cramped little upstairs rooms. The baritone who had played the emperor, man of exquisite feeling and the dispenser of exquisite tortures, a huge fellow in a grubby kerchief and cheeks all pitted with shot, he would run into in another, even less reputable place, where he could be heard grunting, not too musically, behind a thin lath wall.

All this was daily fare and known at every market-stall in the town, but the magic persisted. The moment the lime-lights flared and the velvet curtain went up, these sordid figures, with their dirty fingers and greasy hair, their nick-names, such as the Soup Ladle or the Wismar Eel, were transformed, and what in their lives was crude and shameful, unruly, unredeemable even, was raised, as the music gave shape to it, to ineffable order and beauty – but only insofar as the music did find a shape for it, and only so long as they moved in a world beyond themselves to give it body and a voice. That was a talent, he had to admit, a gift. And those, like himself, who lacked it? What but restraint could redeem them? What but a stern resistance to the destructive power of these emotions, these temptations to disintegration, that brought so much excitement to the nervous system? Wasn't restraint the art of those who lacked a gift? For whom illusionism was too dangerous a drug to be administered save in modest doses between the rise of a curtain and its dusty fall?

These matters he needed to pursue. Late at night, when

the performance was over and half an hour in the smoky hilarity of the town's one brothel had failed to kill in him the deceptive magic and the sweet extravagance of feeling its voices had aroused, he would go back to his room, lay aside the metal accoutrements of his office, strip to the waist, and without lighting a candle, with just the moon for light, wash slowly, almost dreamily, at the wash-stand basin. Then, resuming his shirt, light a candle and fix a reflector, prepare a pen and, seated at the little sloping desk, begin to write: Dear Virgilia . . .

His preparations were a ritual for approaching her. So was the writing. Occasionally, to keep himself grounded, he would push his nose into the sleeve of his shirt, which he had worn all day, and smell stale cigar-smoke, a woman's scented powder, his own sweat. There was no inconsistency between this and the care with which he had sponged his face, his neck, his armpits, his breast – or if there was, it was one he needed. He could write with utter frankness; he had no need, with her, to hide the brutalities of the world he moved in; they would not shock her. What was difficult was the uncovering of his feelings, the exploration of what, once he had expressed it, would be a dangerous fact between them.

Dear Virgilia . . .

'. . . This swooning tendency to disintegration that I find it so necessary, if hard, to resist, is, I know, just what you feel we should surrender to. How many times, over the years, have I asked myself why for you – or so you believe – there is no danger in excess, since only in the intense, the excessive, do our true natures emerge. Are you quite un-afraid of your "true" nature? Can you be so sure of what it is? What if it is monstrous? Is it only because I am less brave than you, less willing to set all at hazard, as these tenors and sopranos do, in the name of a force that takes no heed of what is evil or good or kind or lawful, or conducive to the proper behaviour of citizens, but springs from something further back in us, more obscure, more ancient than the law and all our world of carriage-lamps and roast meat and shaving water; speaks the language of cruelty that we dream in, the language of blood-passion and blood revenge that drives our vocal acrobats to the highest notes in their range and takes them beyond themselves into regions where other rules apply than nature knows or our anxious law-givers – is it only timidity on my part, the cowardice of the man with an overplus of imagination but no gift either to contain or express it, that makes me fly to restraint when I know that even the most rigorous discipline is but the king's hand raised ironically, hopelessly, against the tide . . . ?'

The letters that came in reply were full of excited feeling – of feelings excited by his own, by his need to provoke them. He read feverishly, scanning the pages.

Later, he would go back and savour them, search her phrases for what she might be saying under the bright words she spun out of herself that spoke more, as his did, than they stated. But first he sought something else. For always, slipped in almost as an afterthought, because it would surely interest him, was some mention of Fergus. He waited for it. It was always there. A bald statement, perfectly matter-of-fact among so much extravagant feeling, but he believed, if he put his face to the page, he would feel the extra heat given off by the ink in which she had written: 'Fergus was here on Thursday last and we had a pleasant dinner'; or 'Fergus raced last week at Galway. Won of course, but how could he not, on a splendid new mare?'

It was with the same matter-of-factness that she reported – how long ago – a year, was it only a year? – he was still in Galicia, and could not have guessed what the simple statement would mean, how far it would take him out of his life, though he knew the emotion she must have forced down in herself to write so casually: 'Fergus is gone, no one knows where. Mama Aimée is frantic, as you will no doubt hear. Do you know anything of this?'

His refuge was the profession he had chosen. He was not idealistic. He had no chance to be. Coming into the world after the great epoch of arms, it did not disappoint him, as it did some of his contemporaries, that their generation was to be denied the delirium of victories and disasters that had sown so many fields, from Russia to the Peninsula, with greatcoat buttons, and carried their fathers from the headstrong intoxications of adolescence to a scarred and glorious old age. Nor did it dampen his sense of soldierly pride that he was more often required to see to the needs of his men's stomachs and the state of their feet than to drive them forward in a charge. The military life may be a clinking and jangling business, at least to spectators, but it also has its routine side, which did not entirely displease him. He took a kind of satisfaction in submitting himself to humble duties. They were the refuge. Though he knew that a man who had to be bullied out of his easy acceptance of filth, and would rather be left to wallow, will not thank you for it.

There was in him a need to be of service, to be necessary. It went back, he thought, to the moment in his childhood when he had become the unnecessary adjunct to a household whose only reason for loving or keeping him, unless he created one of his own, was the affection his new mother felt for his old one, the school-friend of her youth. Of the nature of that affection he knew nothing, except that it had survived the twenty years of their separation and the fact that their lives had gone such different ways. Without quite knowing what he was about, he had set out to recreate it; to make himself necessary to Aimée Connellan's heart as his mother had, and in this way not only to find a place of his own there but catch, in whatever affection he could command, the shadow of the mother he could not recall.

Just over six feet tall, Aimée Connellan was known all over the west as the finest horsewoman in the county. She loved her horses, gossip said, better than she loved her husband. This was untrue. She doted on Mr Connellan. Six years her junior, he was a great gambler and notorious womanizer, and, though he was seldom at home, when he did appear, often with a dozen noisy companions who wanted supper, and whiskey and water and a couple of tables for cards, they were so jolly and companionable, fell in so well together, that in the fourteen years of their marriage barely a year had passed when she was not expecting a child. Unhappily, none of them had survived. Ellersley, a small manor house in a hundred and fifty acres, was a house of ghosts, of little names unspoken but recorded in stone behind an iron grille at the end of a Walk. When there were no visitors to dine or play cards or set out on one of the local hunts, the household was a sad one. It had been the business of his coming to brighten it. Even as a child he had recognized that, both the sadness and the light he was expected to spread.

He was a grave little boy, and had come with his own sense of loss, though no one, after his first days in the house, ever mentioned it. All that was asked of him, in that absence of names and faces, was to chatter and be sturdy and to demand as noisily as he pleased a place for himself. The row he made on the stairs, which in another, less haunted household might have been complained of, was looked upon, like his rude health, as a kind of wonder in a house where no child had ever run up and down the basement stairs, or left dirty hand-prints on a wall, or banged with a spoon and said, 'I won't.'

He was recklessly indulged. Not, it is true, by the master and mistress of the house, who were much like children themselves – they seemed afraid of handling him, and when he was brought in to say good-night or to be shown off to visitors, could not always remember what he was called; but the servant girls in the kitchen, when they were not soaking stewpans or peeling potatoes in a bucket of muddy water, were forever snatching him up and trying to cuddle him. Calling him their buttered bun, they would tempt him with bowls of junket to sit on their lap, or haul him dizzy with laughter about the wet floor they were mopping with their skirts up round their legs, or take him off to feed the speckled hens that set their feet down so carefully, so elegantly – 'Look at that one, Lady Muck' – as they strutted about the yard.

But it was not in his nature to be spoiled. He remained soberly withdrawn and was wary of giving himself too freely.

'He's an old-fashioned little lad, isn't 'e?' was how Paddy Mangan put it. 'You are, aren't you, eh? Old-fashioned.'

And he, with a self-important little frown, would answer solemnly, 'Yes, I am,' as if he had given the thing close consideration and come to the conclusion that Paddy Mangan, on the whole, was right.

Paddy did most of the work around the place and was sometimes butler, sometimes coachman (when it was a question only of the cart) and tender of the row of bay-trees and dwarf pomegranates that stood in tubs of Chinese blue-and-white in the marble entrance-hall, which he watered from a can, wearing a special apron. The child liked to trot along in his wake: to watch him, with a green shade over his eyes, take a lock to pieces, oil it, then put it together again, or, sitting in his shirt-sleeves at a sunny bench, mend boots with an awl and waxed thread while the kennel dogs put up a racket at the end of the yard and Mama Aimée's pekinese, Dancer, yapped away on the first-floor balcony; or to help him lubricate the wheels of the carriage, which was seldom used but when it was rolled out of the dark carriage-house, by Paddy and a little gang of grooms and one of the footmen, needed a good deal of attention if it was to meet the demands of the master, whose eye, in all matters of social form, was very precise.

Paddy Mangan was also, though he could neither read nor write, chief counsellor to the lady of the house.

He had come to her from the aunts who had brought her up, Miss Julia and Miss Isabel, and had known Mama Aimée since she was a girl. They had violent quarrels in which Paddy, who always had the upper hand, treated her as if she was still in her aunts' house and nine years old. 'I'm on'y bein' kind,' he told Mrs Upshaw, the housekeeper, who found it scandalous that they should stand, the mistress and this crude old man, shouting at one another in the public hall. 'If I don't rein 'er in,' he explained, 'no one will. She's spoiled. Niver had a word of discipline except what I give her.'

This had been the style of her aunts' house, a generation back, which Mama Aimée had allowed him to carry over into her own because she knew no other.

The aunts, her mother's sisters, had been women of the old sort, untouched by modern notions of primness or sensibility. They had still been alive, though deaf and creaky, when Adair first came to Ellersley. He had been terrified of them. They boomed, wore huge old-fashioned skirts of a brownish rusty colour with a hoop underneath that he had to clamber over to be kissed, and a great many tucks and ribbons, all smelling of stale violets and the snuff they took.

They died within a week of one another, and the wake, which the whole county attended, lasted two days and a night.

One day, coming to the door of his new mother's writing-room, he found her seated at the secretaire with her head in her hands. She was weeping.

He stood at the threshold, gravely absorbed by this demonstration of an emotion that made her different from the person who, till now, he had known only as either very jolly, laughing and exchanging coarse jokes with her husband's friends, or, all exasperation, shouting at Paddy in the hall, or mooning about in the servants' hall where, Mrs Upshaw complained, she made a terrible nuisance of herself, poking into things she knew nothing of – mostly, the servant girls opined, because she was bored to death, poor soul, with that devil of a Mister Connellan away in Dublin chasing after countesses: which did not, Mrs Upshaw insisted, cutting off this sort of insubordinate talk, excuse her wanting to look into the linen cupboard. What would she know about sheets and pillowcases except that they were supposed to smell of lavender and that you slept in 'em?

And now here she was quite changed. With her shoulders in the green silk dress racked with sobs, and the snappish Dancer sitting at her feet with his paws in front of him, very quiet, and his round eyes, in the squashed pug face, fixed upon her. The child leaned in at the door-frame, held back, though he was curious, by the magic that forbade him ever to cross this particular threshold.

It was Dancer who found him and came trotting up. When he leaned down to take Dancer in his arms she raised her head, and Dancer, avoiding him, ran back to her.

'Ah,' she said, 'Michael, it's you.'

She opened her arms and very gingerly he ventured on to the carpet, which was pale and plushy, and she clasped him. She began to weep again, and stroked his hair, and began to tell him things he could make no sense of except that he could feel her hurt, then her anger, then her angry laughter, then her grief, which came back again all in a gust. And all this while, she clasped him tight to her breast and he felt the changes of feeling in the softening of her flesh, or its hardness. He was alarmed to be so close to the source of so much emotion but happy to have her make use of him.

He was not quite four – it was just before Fergus was born.

She acquired the habit, after that, of coming whenever she was troubled and opening her heart to him. He would sit very still, stunned almost to breathlessness by the fierceness of her talk, waiting for the moment when she would again fling herself upon him and squeeze, a thing he dreaded but at the same time hotly longed for. He had learned that so long as her anger lasted, and she kept raging, he would be left to clench his teeth and listen. It was only in the frustration of finding no more words that she would try to impose on him in a more physical way the extremity of her feelings, snatching him up in her arms and forcing her fingers into the bones of his shoulders, splashing hot tears on his neck.

The presence of so much emotion that was not his own, which he wanted to share but was afraid of, made him feel guilty. He wondered if some of her trouble might not have to do with him, with his failure to listen properly to what she was telling him. He would hold himself stiffly, trying to catch, now that there were no more troubling words, some other indication of what it was and what she wanted of him. But his larger guilt was for the moment when he surrendered to her softness, to the voluptuous pleasure of laying his cheek to her breast, of feeling her passionate kisses, as she sobbed, on his ears, his neck, in his hair.

There was also a special smell to these occasions, which he came to associate with her tears and his own pleasurable discomfort. It was a long time before he understood what it was.

'She's been hitting the you-know-what again,' he heard Paddy tell Mrs Upshaw.

'I know what,' the boldest of the girls piped up, Lizzy.

'You know nothing,' Mrs Upshaw told her sharply. 'I'll give you knowing things!'

He looked from one to another of them, trying to catch a clue. Under Mrs Upshaw's eagle eye, the girls were spooning apricots into jars and topping them up with thick yellow liquor, the table before them stacked with columns of light. The girls' faces, which were pallid as usual and none too clean, had the light, he thought, of the sun on them. Wasps, attracted by the syrup, whose sweet smell thickened the air, kept blundering in through the open window and reeling drunkenly round the table or buzzing at the girls' heads, as if they were the source of so much golden sweetness.

'Drat,' Katie cursed. 'Get off me!'

Thwack! She brought a swatter down on the table-top.

Paddy was about to speak again.

'Ears,' Mrs Upshaw warned. 'Big ears,' with a hard look at the girls, '*and* little ears. I'm surprised at you.'

Though free enough with her own complaints and criticisms, the moment anyone else spoke up, she sprang to her lady's defence. She was jealous of Paddy's place in the household, which she found anomalous; it was not what she was used to. It surprised her, considering his lack of formal training and plain ignorance, that he should be such a force. She was very superior. She was trusted with the keys to the tea caddies, administered the sugar lumps, supervised the changing of sheets and pillowcases and bolster-slips. Except in the actual presence of Mama Aimée, when she became tongue-tied with awe, she saw herself so completely as the mistress of the house that she watched every doily or napkin as if it were her own and regarded the brightness of the brass rods that held down the stair-carpets as a measure of her shining influence on the lives of 'the people upstairs'.

She looked at the child to see how much he had grasped of all this. He avoided her eye. Drew patterns with his finger on the pine table-top.

Without knowing it, he had already understood.

Mama Aimée was thirty-eight when Fergus was born, and the household was uncertain for a whole month before whether it was a birth or another funeral they were preparing for. James Connellan arrived and was lovingly attentive, but had little hope that what had failed so often before would succeed on this occasion, and was drunk all week. Though underweight and more than a fortnight premature, the child lived, but they hung back and postponed the celebrations; so long that in the end there were none, not even after the baptism in the little chapel at the end of the Walk.

From the beginning Mama Aimée's attitude to him was fearful and softly guarded. Her fear was that if she showed too much interest he would, like the others, be taken; if she looked too hard at his blue eyes and little perfect fingernails and ears, he would vanish.

She was not a believer but she was powerfully superstitious. There were watchers, spirits born out of the peat bog, creatures with wolf-fangs and withered dugs and thin grey hair who were observing her every movement or look. If they saw how full of need she was, they would work their spell and the boy would sicken. They had to be deceived. She must harden her heart, never look at him except sideways, till he was safe.

And it was true, there was something about the child that was uncanny. He wasn't like a human child – that was the whispered talk among the servant girls, who lived in the same world of folk-tales and old pagan superstitions as their mistress, who had heard this secret lore thirty years ago from peasant girls just like them in her aunts' kitchen.

He never cried.

From the start, too, he would try to catch your eye with his blue one and had in his look all the knowledge of another order of beings, an angel maybe, maybe the opposite.

He was dazzling. It was as if the milk he sucked from the wet nurse turned to light. His skin shone with it.

Only Adair felt free to give the child his unguarded affection. Once he had put on a little strength and could be lifted out of his cradle, he lugged him everywhere; down to the kitchen, to play on the floor while all the daily business of the household was being organized; around the big rooms upstairs, to be shown this or that object that the older child thought might take his fancy: the glass flowers in the depths of a paperweight, the inscription on a sword, the little figures in peasant costume who came out of the barometer – favourites of his own that he hoped might anchor the boy's heart and make him stay.

He had been allowed all this, he saw later, because he was ignorant. Because the watchers, his young mind having no fear of them, had no power over him. So long as he had charge of the child they dared not touch him.

Kitchen lore.

So he had become, in his little old-fashioned way, both brother to Fergus and nurse, and mother and father too;

expert in the recognition of all his needs, and without either embarrassment or fuss, attending to them. Quite soon he was consulted on everything to do with Fergus as if he alone had access to what the child, who was not yet a human child, might demand if he was to settle among them.

But it was no special power he had. Simply that he too was a child, and had for the first time opened his heart and found a language of affection which, so long as that affection was unquestioned, could not be misunderstood.

3

'TELL ME,' ADAIR said, 'is there someone, at home in Ireland maybe, that you want – informed?'

'Informed, sir?'

The man's brow creased. He had not understood. Then he did.

'No, sir, I'm an orphan, sir, I don't reckon as there's anyone would remember me. I was just here an' about like, wanderin'. It weren't a bad life. Except for the dogs.'

But the invocation of Ireland had set something off in him. He sat quiet, dark and brooding.

'Bloody dogs,' he said, under his breath. Then, and the change of tone brought him back into the hut again: 'Ireland's a green place,' he said, as if Adair might never have known it. 'I think sometimes that this place – you know, is a punishment on a man just in itself. Like as if they'd taken Ireland and turned it into a place that made things as hard as they ever could be in this world. I feel sometimes, as if maybe I've never really left it. Just got meself into a part of it, you know, that's meant for those that've gone wrong in life, taken a wrong turning. Could that be it, sir, do you think? When I first come here and see these natives, these black fellers, I thought they was just like us – you know, on'y starved and burned black as a punishment. I thought, so that's what we're in for. Then I thought, maybe if I work me crimes out, or me sins, which is more difficult, I'll just maybe wake up one mornin' and there it'll be, all fresh and green, the old country. I'll be back. Well, it never happened of course.' He sat, staring again into the dark before him. 'It's a fearful place, sir. You must feel that.'

'And why,' Adair said with a touch of humour, 'do you think I am here? For what sins committed?'

The man was taken aback. 'I wouldn' know that, sir,' he said at last. 'It's for each man to say for himself. An' get out as best he can.'

'And did you really believe that? That this place is just Ireland in another way of thinking? An Ireland that has gone bad?'

'I told you, sir, I'm ignorant, I didn' know what to think. I was tryin' to explain to meself. Why one place should be so green and like, easy – if it was hard too, at times – and the birds so – well sir, you know what the birds was. Larks an' that, yaffles – I loved them birds. It must mean something, I thought, that this place should be so dry and cursed, with nothin' in sight that a man can get a handle on, an' every day so hard. Was that wrong then? Was there never any way of gettin' back? For any of us?'

'I don't say that. – I don't know, Carney,' he said at last. 'You ask me things I can't answer. A man can do anything he wants, if he puts his mind to it. Or so they tell us.'

'Do they, sir? Well,' he said slowly, 'a lot of what they tell us turns out to be untrue. That's what I found. Bloody lies, in fact. Even an ignorant man will find that out. Sooner or later.'

Adair smiled to himself. Did the fellow think he had not?

'It's hard enough tryin' to find out the way things are, without they bloody lie to us as well.'

'Do you always tell the truth then?'

'No sir, I do not, an' I'll admit it. But I had to get by, sir, an' how else could I do it? I had me skin to save.'

'Every man has his skin to save.'

'Is that right, sir? Even them as has power?'

'Oh yes, those most of all.'

'Well then! I thought they would of been safe and easy. I thought their lyin' was just a way of holdin' us down – you know, keepin' us ignorant. And poor.'

Adair looked hard at the man. There was a moment of silence.

'Can I ask you, sir? – I told you what I think of this country. Maybe it's what a man like me would think, considerin', an' isn't the truth. I mean, it was always a punishment to me, an' that's how I took it. But you, sir. What is it to you? You're free to leave any time you like. But you're here.'

What could he answer? That it had been imposed upon him too? Not as a punishment but in ways that were equally inescapable. How to explain, save by beginning on a story there was no time to finish and might have no end, it went back so far and involved so many byways of feeling that to another would be inexplicable; a rigmarole of incomprehensible motives, misguided folly, hopeless reachings after what from the beginning was already lost, all the confused and indirect ways by which he had come to a place ten thousand miles from where he began – to this particular spot in it, this moment when a stranger to whom he had, after all, nothing to say, could give him a straight look and ask.

But what the man said was true. Here he was, and some quality of the country, some effect of the high clear skies, so unlike the skies of Ireland, that raised the ceiling of the world by pushing up the very roof of your skull, had got into his head and changed his sense of what lay before, and behind too. So much space, so much distance under the dry air, had opened his eyes to the long view, as even the great plains of Poland, in the years he served there, had not, since these distances were empty, with no roads across them, no prospect of a village up ahead, however mean, with muddy alleys where pigs wallowed, and rotten fences and white-washed huts with the dome of a little wooden church over all; only a high, wide emptiness that drew you on into an opening distance in yourself in which the questions that posed themselves had no easy sociable answer, concerned only yourself and what there was at last, or might be, between you and the harsh, unchanged and unchanging earth, and above, the unchanged, unchangeable stars.

Three days ago, riding across the coastal plain towards the foothills of the Range, he had passed farms where they were bringing in the harvest.

A dry country, it's true; yellow, burned-looking, not lush like home. But the earth had taken the unaccustomed seed. It had sprouted, broken ground, shot up, thickened, been reaped, and was now being laid out in bundles in stubble-fields. Men and women, small children too, were staggering over the land with great stooks in their arms, to lean them one against the other and make, in a place that had never known such a thing in all of previous time, a scene, busy, productive, that had at first glance the immemorial order of a landscape at home, till you raised your eyes and saw what a tiny patch of order it was in the surrounding bush and against the jagged wilderness of the mountains beyond.

He had heard, as he passed, the voice of a little girl calling: 'Dadeeee . . .', a rope of breath rising and looping through the air; and long after he had begun the climb into the foothills, above the strange tinking of bellbirds, the echo of it stayed with him. It hung on in his head, but changed, as he turned away, into the cry of a raven, and he thought again, less sentimentally now, of the land he had grown up in. A sorrowful land, with the fine rain thin as smoke blow-ing in from the Atlantic so that the taste of it was there on your lip, the smell of it in sheets that had been laid over a bush to dry. Salt and sorrow over the fields, a sad country; mournful, made human by the long sorrows it had endured, the sorrows yet to come.

Many of those families down there were ones whose menfolk, back home on the other side of the world, poor tenant farmers or day-labourers, would have had no prospect in all eternity of owning even an acre of land, and here they were offered hundreds if they had the strength to tear it out of the wilderness and plough and work it. That surely was something.

The huts that stood off in the distance were dirt-floored cabins, one-roomed, windowless, but might one day, if the seasons were kind, be replaced with houses of cut stone such as the better sort of farmers had already established, and the children who turned to watch him pass, wiry boys and long-legged little girls who raised their tanned faces and pale hands, would have a life that was unimaginable to their cousins at home, who were still cutting peat or driving cows into a shitty byre or watching sheep in a glen among flattened heather. It might fail, all this. But then again, it might not.

What did he think of this country? It wasn't one. It was a place that was still being made habitable. A venture, another example of the inextinguishable will of men and women to make room for themselves, some patch of the earth, however small, where they could stand up, feel the ground under their feet and say, This is mine, I have made it, I have made it mine. A place where they could lie down too and make children and say, This is yours, I am giving it to you, in trust. A place where a family could come to the table and pass from hand to hand dishes with food on them, mutton, potatoes, that they had made the land yield up to them, the loaf with the knife beside it and the thick slices handed round, which was seed they had planted, fat grains they had rolled between thumb and forefinger while they looked up anxiously at the sky, a weight of stooks they had lugged over the field to lean one against the other in the old pattern while the sweat ran down into their eyes and dust and sweat ran down from their armpits.

What did he know of this country? Better ask those who had set their lives down here and would risk the venture. He was a stranger here, a passer-by. He would go eventually and not come back. He had no right to speak.

Some of this he might have said to Carney, but the man's mind, moving back, had already moved elsewhere. He sat now, hunched in thought. At last he said:

'Thank you, sir.'

'For what?'

'For bein' truthful with me. I appreciate it.'

'I'm no more truthful than any other man. I mean, Carney,' he said more gently, 'you should trust no one. No one.'

'I see, sir. Very well, sir.' He did not point out that wise as this advice might be, he would have little chance to make use of it. At last, after a long silence he spoke again.

'Can I tell you something, sir?'

'Of course.'

'When you asked, sir, if there was anyone as should be told, I suppose you meant, was there anyone would have a memory of me. Well, there isn't no one to be told, but there is someone who might, every now and again, keep a memory of me. Not of me exactly – me name, I mean. I don't believe they would ever of known that. But of – ' His hand moved vaguely to indicate what might have been his body, or some other more nebulous entity that hovered around it, of which his chest and shoulders were the only thing he could point to that could evoke its existence.

'I was in the town of Limerick – do you know it, sir? I don't much, I only been there the once. I was in the market-place, you know – waitin' for work. Standin' there alongside of a lot of other fellers. It was a raw, cold day, just before Christmas, and we was all huddled together like, stampin' our feet and huggin' ourselves to keep warm. Waitin' to be chosen. That's how it happens, sir, in case you don't have experience of it. You stand there and the farmers come, or the stewards if it's a big place, an' they look you over like, to see what you might be good for. I never had much fear I wouldn' be chose. I was young then, not more 'n twenty I reckon, an' big, as you see. An' I'd learned the trick of it by then. It was best, you know, to look – as if you wouldn' give trouble. I didn't normally wait long, an' I didn't this time, neither. Two fellers come right up to me and says: "You. Come on." I didn' like it much. I seen them standin' apart, sort of lookin' me over in a way I didn' like, and they chose just the one of us. That's odd, I thought. Still, what could I do? I was there to be hired. I couldn' do nothing but follow.

'We went round to the yard of an inn where there was a trap waitin', and we drove about six miles into the country-side. It was cold. The one feller, he was all in brown, had a rug over his knees, the other not. I sat shiverin'. I remember it was all snow once you got beyond the last of the muddy streets o' the town, and there was more to come, just hanging there, waitin' to fall – you know how it is, sir, the ground cold but the air somehow warmish. You know then that there's snow about. And the light – everything has a touch of blue to it. That's the sort of day it was.

'Anyway, we come at last to a set of gates and a drive round a circle in front of a house, and the one feller throws the rug off and jumps down and says: "Tilley'll look after you." Tilley was older, with grey whiskers.

'We went round the back, into a yard with pools of frozen milk between the pavin's and a great stack o' dung in one corner, black and smoking, an' a feller goin' at it with a pitchfork, that turned and stared at me, curious like, and a little barefoot lad leading a bull with a ring through its nose that was lifting its head and roaring so that breath come out of its nostrils. It was pulling against the rope and the little lad had his heels dug in, cursing.

' "Get on," Tilley shouted, and the feller on the dungheap turned away and began to pitch into the pile, but still had an eye on me – I knew that sideways, sly look, I could tell. An' the little lad was stopped still, staring.

'What's this? I thought.

'We come to the kitchen. There was a woman there, oldish, an' a young one come out from under the stairs. Tilley said: "This feller'll need a bath and a new set of clothes."

'I wanted to ask what work I was to do, but the old 'un just shrugged 'er shoulders and told the young 'un to bring out the tub, then looked at me, hopeless like – I was all rags – and said: "All right, lad, get them things off."

'When I stopped a minute, you know, shy like, she laughed and said: "What do you think? That we'll be lookin' at you? Molly, will you want to be lookin' at the lad t' see what 'e's got?" The girl went red in the face. "No, missus," she said, "not me. I wouldn' look if you paid me. I'm scared t' look at 'im at all." "So then," the old girl says, "get yerself ready and I promise I won't make the water too hot."

'So I stripped meself, and then, when she'd filled the tub I climbed in an' the old 'un washed me hair and took a scrubbin' brush to me back an' all – I was niver so clean in all me life – an' I put on the clothes they brought. Which was a gentleman's clothes, and they fit me pretty well except

57

for the shoes, which pinched, I could hardly get into 'em. A white shirt, which someone had been wearing, but that didn' worry me. No jacket. Then the old 'un combed me hair and stood back and give me a weird look and laughed, and said: "Just as well she's blind, poor darlin'." But the young 'un did not laugh. "God help 'er," she said, and would not look at me. "Go wan," the old 'un said when she had looked me over again. "Through there."

'She pushed me out into a dark low little passageway, all wooden walls, and an old 'un, another, all in black, was sittin' there on a little three-legged creepie workin' a pair a' needles. She looked me up and down and made a little like laughing sound in her throat and shouted. "Tilley!"

'He come out of a low door. "Stand back," he said.

'He looked me over and did not look pleased. Then he turned back into the door: "The feller, sir."

'It was the gentleman, the one in brown. He was sitting at a desk and peering up at me through a pair of round little glasses.

' "Well," he said, "here's a change."

'He got up and walked round me once, then again, then stood with his hands behind his back, silent like, considerin'. Then sat back down again.

' "You shall have a sovereign," he says. "That's a great deal of money. Do you know how much that is?"

' "Yes, sir, I do," I says.

' "Do you read at all?" he asks me. I admitted I did not. "Good," he says. "You will forget what happens here today, do you understand that? One shilling of the sovereign is for what you will have to do, which is nothing much. To stand for five minutes and do and say nothing. Whatever happens, you stand still and hold your tongue. Understood? The rest of the sovereign, that is nineteen shillings out of the twenty, you get for doing even less. For forgetting you have ever been here. One shilling for one kind of silence, nineteen for the other."

'He gave a little laugh at that, but it was not for my benefit, the little joke he made. He thought I would not understand it.

' "Now, you know your part, all you have to do is play it. You stand still and say nothing. Can you manage that? And the sovereign – here it is, safe and sound in my breast pocket – you shall have to go away with, immediately after," and he dropped the coin, which was a bright new one, into the pocket of his waistcoat and patted it, and smiled. But Tilley did not. He coughed and looked at his boots, and we all stayed quiet till the brown man pulled his chair back and said, "Very well Tilley. Might as well begin. And remember, you, from this time on, not a word!"

'They led me back into the hallway where the old woman with the needles sat over her knitting, then through a door at the end into a kind of parlour that looked out to the lawn.

'What struck me was the whiteness. Snow! The gleam of it through the low window hit me clean between the eyes. The whole room was lit.

'There was an old lady there with a lot of clothes on and a wig that didn't fit and a walkin' stick. She was sort of spread out wide all over a little sofa where she sat leaning forward on the stick. An' stood in the winder with her back to us was another, a child I thought it was, she was that little. But as soon as she heard us come in she turned – it was a young girl – and looked right at me, but in such a strange way I thought she might be simple like. "What is it?" she said, and stood there with her lips a little apart. "Has he come?"

'I see then that she was blind.

'We all stood very quiet, me an' the brown man an' Tilley.

An' the old lady in the wig looked at her, tragic like, an' shook her head, an' looked at the brown man, an' he lifted a finger, just the one, like this, warnin' her to be quiet, an' she shook her head again an' looked at her lap. The girl was just stood still in the middle of the room.

'She was young, and very little, undergrown like, and pale.

'The brown man made a sign to me to stand still, then he took the girl's arm, just here under the elbow, and at the same time give me a look and lifted his chin, which meant I should lift my chin. Which I did, and still didn' know what else I should do, so I just stood. On'y me heart started up, I don't know why. In a minute it was beatin' so fast it was like I was running, running away from somethin', dead scared. It was beatin' so hard I could hear it, an' I thought they must of been able to hear it too – how could they miss it? I thought – an' when the brown man, with just a little shove like, set 'er loose, I thought she 'ud find me by that, by the way me heart was going. But from the way she raised her head I knew she was smelling me out – the way a dog would. It's a strange thing, that is – I can't tell you. I thought, this won't work, she'll smell the difference. She must. You see, sir, I was beginnin' to sweat. She'll smell that, I thought, but what can I do about it? They didn' pay me not to sweat. She come very close then and put 'er face into me shirt – her head come just to me breast here – and I felt the breath go out of 'er and a shiver went over me.

'She put 'er hand up then and her fingers touched me. She felt round the shape of me ear. This one. Then across me cheek and down to the corner of me lip. Over the top one, then back acrost the bottom, then into the hollow place under it.' – His rough hand as he spoke was moving over the broken features.

'Well, I just shut me eyes and let 'er. It was like lyin' still,

60

you know, in the dark, an' lettin' some creature – I don't know what it might be – walk over your face, and you with no power to cry out or brush it away. But it was gentle like. She was searchin' me out. Tryin' to discover who it was. This is a strange thing, I told meself. It's like a dream.

'I kept me eyes shut like I was asleep, trying to keep me balance there in them shoes, holdin' me breath. And her hand went back to me ear, and across me face again, and down to me lips.

'I'd never thought about me ear – not really *thought*. It was just there. But when her touch went all over it I felt it sort of light up, like, and glow. Me lips the same. They swelled up, I could feel the blood in them. Then her fingers went to the other ear, the right one. Then down me neck into me shirt, which was open, to the bit of gristle here in me throat, and I swallowed and it jumped up, an' I had to clear me throat, an' the brown man must of thought I was goin' to speak, I felt him stir, an' I opened me eyes, an' she stepped back an' was frowning at me. There was a little crease, just here, between her brows.

'I'd sort of felt, while I had me eyes shut, there was just the two of us. Both out in a field somewhere, or a wood it might be, in the dark. But I seen then that the others was there, all watchin'.

'Her head come forward. I seen the parting in the top of her head. She puts her nose into me shirt.

'I was beginnin' to sweat bad by now. She'll know now, I thought. When her face touched my skin another shiver went over me – she felt it and a little smile come to her lips. She stood like that for a long time, breathin' in the smell of me – was she fooled? – an' I looked across and saw the old lady had a lace handkerchief to her lips, and tears runnin' down her cheeks, an' the truth was, I was upset and – There was something else as well. I mean, I'd stiffened up, if you know what I mean, an' I was ashamed to have to stand there with them others watchin' where they could see it. Me stiff cock, if you'll excuse the expression sir, standin' up in them tight pants they'd put me in.

'Her face was close. I could look right into it. Tears had come into her eyes an' I watched 'em spill over and start to run down her cheeks. She give a kind of groan, an' then her hand went for me, for me cock, an' felt it, that it was stiff, an' she sort of collapsed against me – I nearly cried out then – an' started to sob, an' the old lady's mouth opened, an' the brown man pulled her away, an' she was beginnin' to cry out something terrible – it went right through me, I felt so sorry for her grief, or her disappointment, I don't know what it was. She started to struggle and scream out, an' I could still hear 'er when Tilley got me out of the room and the door shut behind us. A terrible sound, sir, I can hear it still. I was shakin' so much I could hardly stand.

'Well, they took me back to the kitchen and give me me dinner. You'd think maybe I couldn' eat after all that. I thought I couldn't neither, I felt that low. It was roast beef, a good thick slice, with gravy and potaters. I did eat it. I didn' know where I'd get a better feed. There was a pudding and I ate that too. The ol' girl who'd washed me didn' have much to say now and the young 'un wouldn't look at me.

'Afterwards the brown man come and give me the sovereign, and they give me the clothes to go away in, with me own wrapped up in a bit of paper. The shoes too. But they was no good to walk in, so I sat under a hedge and took 'em off, and sold them later for six shillings. So I did well enough. But it wasn't a day's work I was proud of. It worried me. Like I don't know to this day who it was – a dead man maybe – they had me play, and what they were getting out of it, out of foolin' her, I mean, the feller in brown whose sovereign I took, the ol' lady. And why me? When they come into the market and looked around like, why it was me they took.

'Afterwards I thought a lot about that. I'd go over an' over it. I'd lie in the dark, like, and touch me ear the way she did. This one. Then run me hand over the cheek, then the top lip, then the bottom. The truth is, no one ever touched me like that, sir, either before nor after. Then I'd hear that terrible cryin' an' wonder what it was I'd done to 'er.

'Something else, as well. I used to feel sometimes, that when she searched me out like that she might of discovered something – an' I wonder what. I'd have give the sovereign back, I reckon, ten times over, to know. I only drank it away. I'd like – you know, to ask 'er. If she's still alive, poor soul, and has kept a memory of it. Which she must do, surely, don't you think, sir? Because it would of meant more to her. Though it meant something to me too, even if it wasn't intended that way. Our life is a strange thing, sir, don't you think? Well, I don't know that that's a question, exactly – You'll be glad, sir.' He gave a wet laugh. 'One less to answer.'

4

WHEN HE WAS five, with Paddy in a frieze coat to drive him, he was sent two miles away to the Park, to learn his letters with the daughter of a local landowner, and Mama Aimée's great friend, Eamon Fitzgibbon – a practical arrangement and an excellent opportunity since this idiosyncratic gentleman had decided that his daughter, the child of a late second marriage, should have the same education he had given to the three grown-up sons of the first. She was a bright little girl, a few weeks older than Adair, called Virgilia, who when he arrived already knew her letters and could read a little. Instead of intimidating or mocking, she encouraged him to catch up, and from that point on they did everything together.

Blue-eyed, red-haired, with an easy athletic style to the way she carried herself, she was not a tomboy, not at all; but her father treated her exactly as he had treated his sons. She had nothing about her of the falsely demure. Encouraged to speak up for herself, even among her father's guests, where she very competently played hostess, she was quite certain of her place in the world, and when Adair was inclined to fall behind, soon got him going again with her own fierce example. He had no idea, till she confessed her own, that he should have an ambition.

'I think I shall be a soldier,' he told her innocently. He was eight years old.

Perhaps it was because she knew it was a field that was

barred to her that she gave him such a withering answer: 'You might at least have said a general.'

It was his first apprehension of the difference between them.

He was always aware of limits. Not because he was timid, or out of modesty, or even because reasonableness was so much part of his nature, but because he had already come to understand that his position was an anomalous one. He might be treated like a little lord, but he had no natural rights, no assured title or place. He was dependent on the kindness, the charity, of others, and on what he could do in the way of service, or command in the way of affection, to keep it. This was humiliating. Though he had never been made to feel it, he was acute enough to have discovered all this for himself, and suffered, though without resentment. It also meant that he could take nothing in his life as given.

Virgilia accepted no limits, either to the wildness of her imaginings or to her own capacity to make them real. He thought she was wrong in this. His understanding of his position, he thought, made him wiser than she was or less trusting. There grew up in him a belief, it was his one great secret, that when she too discovered the truth of things, when she had broken herself on the hard facts of the world, she would find her best comfort in him.

What she had determined upon was the role of lady traveller in Morocco or the Morea or the plains of Anatolia, or to lead a party into the jungles of West Africa. Her mind, in a way that astonished him, had already moved beyond the Park, and Oughterard, and even Dublin, and he wondered if it wasn't this, some sense in which she brought back from the places her imagination moved to a vision of desert wastes under the moon, of equatorial heat and a sky continuously alive with lightning, that made him at times a little afraid of her, as well as for her; as if what she had in her head might be more real to her than the things they were surrounded by and from which he, in his stolid way, took so much comfort: the chalk in the knuckles of his square, rather stumpy fingers; the nails in his boots; the ticks and crosses in his exercise book that marked a sum either right or wrong; but also the cart with its yellow splashboard that took him back and forth under rain so fierce and slashing at times that it was like shining gravel flung at your face, and seagulls squatting white in the furrows like unseasonable snow, and on other occasions, real snow, dirty white, fretted and frozen on the ridges, with ravens wheeling above it like scavenger spirits unloosed from graveyards, filling an unforgiven world with their savage cry. He was sober and practical. Weighed down not only by his boots, the dirt under his nails, the landscape of potato-clamps and flashes of boggy water that was reflected in his eyes, but in his accepting all this, as Virgilia did not, as the grounds of his nature.

Nothing made this more plain than the difficulty he had with a side of Virgilia that from the beginning both disturbed and confused him: the lies she told.

At first he was merely confused. She was testing him, to see how far she could go before he would stand up to her.

But she had on these occasions such an excited glow, was so full of imperious assurance, that though his mind said, This is a story, she's making it up, he drew back from challenging her outright. There was something in him that wanted the stories, since they meant so much to her, to be true.

They were all of encounters, on walks out from the Park, with strangers no one else had ever laid eyes on, though they must have been conspicuous enough on roads where the only traffic was labourers going to and from the fields and the occasional wagon or cart.

Once it was a troupe of acrobats in yellow and blue silk pyjama-suits, who were chattering to one another as they walked in what she took to be Chinese. They turned off into a clearing, strung a rope between two trees, and went walking up and down on it carrying parasols which they opened, tossed in the air, and caught twirling on a fingertip.

On another occasion it was an Italian lady who had been put out of a passing carriage and was sitting, with all her luggage about her, on a camp-stool in the shade of an elm. She had a negro with her, a little pageboy all in white; they were playing cards. She was waiting, but not in an anxious way, for the lover she had offended to think better of it and come back. Meanwhile, she and the little negro were enjoying their game, slapping down their cards and insulting one another, but were delighted, when she turned up, to have some new diversion. The little negro unpacked another stool from one of the lady's trunks and brought them lemonade in silver cups. When the carriage, as the lady had predicted, came rolling back, she gave Virgilia a farewell present of a musical box in the shape of a scollop shell, which she refused to show him, and a silver coin with the head of the King of Naples on it, which she did – but he had seen it before.

'You don't believe me, do you?' she demanded. 'Well, do you?'

But how could he? His notion of the truth was firm and unblinking but he could not look her in the eye. Instead he looked at his boots, and saw in their roundness what it was that she was challenging in him: his refusal to do what she was doing, to take flight from dusty reality and make their dull world yield up wonders. That was why she told only lies that he would immediately recognize; with her fierce integrity she would have despised a lie that was intended to deceive. The world must conform – that is what she was claiming – to her own high demands of it.

But lies, his hob-nailed, earthbound nature insisted, were lies. The world would *not* conform. And what then? Virgilia's, he thought, was a dangerous principle; even if what impelled it was a spirit of idealism, the wish that life should be larger, wilder, more curious than it was.

And wasn't she wrong even in this?

Mary McGee, one of their maids at Ellersley, had a brother who was nine years old and had never been out of bed. His head, which was the size of a pumpkin, was so heavy that the wizened stalk of his body could not carry it about.

Dinny McManus, the son of the Park gamekeeper, had shown them a fairy-ring in the field they called the Fianna's Ground just at the entrance to the woods: a perfect circle of mushrooms in which fairies danced.

In Pennsylvania, Benjamin Franklin had collected an electric charge from a cloud. It was a new kind of power. One day, Eamon Fitzgibbon had told him, houses, whole towns would be lighted with it, and the light would be of an intensity no man had ever seen, more than a thousand candles worth. Even the brightest day would not match it.

They took their lessons in the Schoolroom, which was in the second storey of the Park and close enough to the Library for Eamon Fitzgibbon to drop in, sometime towards noon, to see how they were progressing and to quiz them in front of their tutor about what they had learned.

The Schoolroom looked out on to a lawn where the branches of a great dark cedar of Lebanon reached almost to the ground. While you were waiting for the answer to come, or simply day-dreaming, you could crawl into the dark maze of roots there where no one could reach you, and tumble about in the skin of a vole, with a vole's tiny heart-beat.

Sometimes, fallow deer came right up to the wall where the Italian garden was laid out, an intricate geometry of box hedges and fragrant herbs. They stood very still like statues and you held your breath. They raised their heads, motionless, intent, as if the answer Mr Meecham was waiting for were being whispered out there on the still air and all you had to do was freeze, hold your breath, be all attention as they were, to get wind of it.

Mr Meecham was a red-faced Englishman with watery blue eyes and a pinched nose encrimsoned by the over-use of snuff. His face above his starched cravat went steadily darker on these occasions. He furrowed his brow with the effort of getting the answer out of his own head into yours; pushed his lips forward to offer a hint of the first consonant, though they declined to read it. Virgilia, especially, despised him for being so anxious, and might have punished him by deliberately giving a wrong answer, but was too proud to pretend to an ignorance she did not suffer from, or to deceive her father in a thing that meant so much to him. The limit of her malice was to keep poor Mr Meecham swelling and teetering; though sometimes this holding back had another reason, which was to give *him* the chance to answer, since he too at times grew anxious under the old man's stern and, he felt, unforgiving gaze, or stumbled out of shyness, so that what he knew quite well flew clean out of his head.

The belief that he had got the answer before her made him secretly triumphant. When he saw the truth he was doubly humiliated. Only then did he see that a characteristic generosity and largeness of spirit always took precedence over her vanity or the wish to insist on a superiority that had no need of proof. This amazed him since he found nothing like it in himself.

'So then,' Paddy would ask as they drove away, 'what did they learn ye this time?' And he would retail to Paddy some of the facts the tutor had passed on to them, things that made Paddy puzzle and scratch his head.

In the early days he had been patronizing.

'Well, ye're right there,' he'd say, 'that's the truth, they're not tellin' you any lie. On'y I thought you would of known that, Master Mick. *I* did. I'd of told you it meself if I'd of known you didn't. I could've been your schoolmaster, what d'e say to that, eh?' And he laughed. 'So what else did they tell yer?'

But later, when they got on a little, he changed his tune.

'Well, is that true now, who'd of thought it? Tell it to me again, lad, slow like. It's hard that, I don't think I've got hold of it. Maybe it won't go into me thick skull. Try me agin.'

He was reluctant, the boy saw with a little surge of affection, to have him pass out of a stage where they could be on terms of equal understanding.

Later, in the pantry where they were decanting wine, he would hear Paddy, in a lordly way, instructing Gerald, the new footman, in something he had till just that afternoon been entirely ignorant of but which now filled his mind as if he had always known it, and which he presented to the footman as a thing he had better knock into his head pretty smartly if he meant to *get* anywhere.

But it could not go on.

'I'll tell you something, Mickey, darlin',' he confessed one day when he had let Adair take the reins, 'just between you and me like. I know you won't hold it against me.' He rubbed hard the end of his nose with the heel of his hand. 'I cannot read, it's a great grief to me. I niver learned. I'll niver know what's in them books you traipse back 'n forth unless you tell it to me. It'd be a real charity, me love, if one day you took the trouble and learned me me letters. Would you do that for your ol' Paddy? It'd be a real satisfaction to me to be able to read a little in one o' them books before I go to me grave.'

To the amazement of the girls, and the wonder of Mrs Upshaw, they sat at the kitchen table, the seven-year-old boy and the man of nearly sixty, and puzzled it out. By the end of the year, with his glasses at the end of his nose, Paddy could work his way through one or two paragraphs of the newspaper. 'I don't reckon,' he told the boy with a grin, 'that I need go on to Latin. You can tell me about that, love. I'll stick to English. There's enough in that, I dare say, to keep me goin'.'

He and Virgilia had gone on to Latin. And Greek.

They still took their lessons with Mr Meecham, but when they were finished with mathematics and spelling and the globe, they went off to the big dim library where the gold, leather-bound volumes on the shelves glowed like the trunks of a forest, and on the ceiling overhead Mnemosyne sat looking smug at the head of a committee of pert blue-stockings, her nine pink-mouthed, small-breasted daughters. There, Eamon Fitzgibbon, in a plain cravat like a French-man, took them patiently through their conjugations. They read about the schoolmaster of Falerii, how a good charm for thunder and lightning can be made out of a mixture of onions, hair and pilchards, and how Remus saw six vultures but Romulus twice as many, and how, since then, the Romans, in their divination by the flight of birds, chiefly observe the vulture since 'it is a creature the least mischievous of any, pernicious neither to corn, plants nor cattle, and neither kills nor preys upon anything that has life, and as for birds, does not touch them even when they are dead because they are of its own nature, whereas eagles, owls and hawks tear and kill their own kind' – 'Like men,' Eamon Fitzgibbon added. 'And how many great men, nobles and patriots, do we see choosing the vulture as their emblem?'

He was a more patient teacher than Mr Meecham. He knew more of a child's mind, and for all his austere nature, was more inclined to make a game of their lessons and to joke. Adair, quite soon, was no longer afraid of him. He was inducting them, like an old magician, into a world that was all oddness and enchantment, but one too where the virtues he admired could be seen in their ideal form and where Virgilia, and the boy too in time, would discover the perfect examples of what, without quite knowing it, they already aspired to and had begun to play out in their games. Adair became a great favourite with the old man, who saw in the boy's earnest and curious nature, his devotion to duty, his rigorous self-control, but also perhaps in some darker aspects which he also recognized, his ideal offspring, the child – sprung fully formed into the world – of his own moral nature. And in this Virgilia, though she remained the cleverer of the two, acquiesced. Her power over each of them, in every other area of their lives, was absolute.

The Park and its many dependencies was modelled on the Roman villa. A marvel of order and economy, it was a monument as well to the owner's love of fantasy and play.

Eamon Fitzgibbon's passion for engineering had gone into the hydraulic works that drained the boggy soil for the home farm and created a lake and a string of fish-ponds, but also into decorative waterworks and, in a grotto made of fan after fan of shells brought all the way from Sicily, a series of fountains that struck up as you approached, through a clockwork mechanism, a set of minuets and Turkish marches, and when you got close enough shot a jet of water in your face.

Clockwork.

Adair loved the part that clocks played in the life of the Park.

Everything there was timed to the last minute. Clocks were everywhere. There was no corner of the place, he sometimes thought, where you were out of the sound of their ticking. They were the true gods, the Lares and Penates, of the household: tall ones in walnut cases, with a copper sun and moon on the face, mantel clocks in gilt ormolu, upheld by sinuous nymphs and youths all muscle, that sat on marble-topped commodes and mantel-pieces and occasional tables inlaid with flowers in *pietra dura*; water clocks, carriage clocks in which you saw all the flywheels and little copper rods at work under a glass dome, convenient timepieces in the pocket of all the Park servants, who soon learned that promptness, a proper attention to the hour, was the local style of worship, a tribute to the great organizer of the universe, which was also a kind of clock, though it was to the Bréguet watch in their master's waistcoat-pocket that their own was synchronized, which was the heart of their own little universe and to whose ticking their ear, their attention, their every gesture was distantly attuned. Throughout their lesson it sat on the Riesener desk at Eamon Fitzgibbon's elbow, and all the activities of a great enterprise, in granary and mill and icehouse and chandlery, in the kitchen with its cauldrons and turning spits, out in the fields where scythes flashed and whistled and women were gathering and binding sheaves or giving their children a breast in the shade of a whitethorn hedge, were timed and measured as they revolved about it.

But time was not an enemy at the Park, to be warred with and buried under a pile of empty trophies. The aim of life, Eamon Fitzgibbon preached, was Freedom and Joy. To use time well, he believed, frees us, and Freedom and Joy in the end are one.

As a youth of sixteen, he had been on the Grand Tour and, already master of the Park, had brought back paintings and marbles of every sort to make the place beautiful as well as habitable, but also a great many fragments of bone, knuckle-bones and vertebrae, that were the remains of real Romans and had come out of their tombs and were laid out now, annotated by his own hand, in cases behind glass.

Educated in France, he had gone back at the time of the Revolution, and it was Robespierre he spoke of with the warmest admiration and regret, another vulture perhaps, and in the same way slandered and misrepresented, he explained, by common minds.

On formal occasions, as when he came in a phaeton with the apron back to pay his respects to Mama Aimée on her birthday, or in a closed carriage at New Year, he wore a powdered wig, but otherwise his dress was the plain one of a citizen, his reddish-grey hair in a loose knot, an eye-patch over his left eye, which made the right one, Adair thought, which was a startling blue but rimmed with blood, all the more commanding. In the ideal landscape of his dreams, it hung over the misty fields, round, ever watchful, like a fierce but beneficent sun.

Before long Fergus too made the trip each day to the Park. Not yet as a scholar, he was too young for that, but because he would not allow the older boy out of his sight, and because there was nowhere else for him to go. He soon became another element in the life there. They took it in turns to rock or comfort him but it was Adair who cared for the child's physical needs.

Virgilia's idea of motherhood involved a good deal of petting and pampering, the chanting of nursery-songs and the organization of games in which Fergus learned pretty early to do what she required of him but when he went still, made a face, reddened, and Adair said solemnly, 'He's filling his pants,' Virgilia looked aggrieved. She retired to a safe distance behind a table, and it was Adair who, efficiently and with no feeling of distaste – he was used to it – lay the child gently down, cleaned up his mess and changed him.

Fergus during these ministrations lay very still and trusting under his hands, and from the corner of his eye Adair observed, not without a kind of humorous satisfaction, the look of mild disgust with which Virgilia followed his movements. But there was curiosity there and envy too. She must see, he thought, how these moments of intimacy pleased him. How completely, while he worked, Fergus was his.

Occasionally, when this was too clear, or when he was too smugly absorbed in the little sing-song encouragements and endearments he used to get Fergus to turn this way and that, and which involved a whole secret language between them, she would grow scornful and mock him.

'What a good little mother it is,' she would sing. 'Isn't it a good little mother he is?'

But he did not care. Quite the opposite, it pleased him. The fact was, he could scarcely remember a time now when Fergus had not been there, hanging on his hip or crawling in to cuddle against him in their nursery bed: like an extension of himself, a part of his nature he had not known existed till it appeared in this close, imperative form, this little other being with its own hard or yielding will, that insisted on being carted about or set on his shoulders to crow over the table-tops and the jaws of snappy pekinese, and who, after a time, took up all his affection, all the unused tenderness towards the world that made him open not only towards Fergus but to every sort of small and helpless creature, the kittens that appeared in a corner of the kitchen and which, for all his pleading, Paddy took off in a sack to be drowned, puppies, calves, the weak-kneed, new-born foals they went to the stables to see dragged, long legs first, out of mares laid trembling in the straw, and which from the beginning, he could not have said why, he associated with Fergus, who watched big-eyed from between his knees.

He was changed, he felt, by this new presence, so much so that it was inevitable after a time that the world he moved in should also change, and most of all the one he and Virgilia had created.

Till now there had been just the two of them, and for a while after Fergus began to come to the Park, to play on the floor of the Schoolroom while they did their lessons, or hug Adair's knee, they remained two. Only when Virgilia began to involve Fergus in the games she devised did their world open to include the boy as more than an acceptable nuisance.

He provided his own little centre of interest, had his own way of going about things and of finding what it was in the world that shone out and demanded to be seen – things they had not noticed till he touched them and took them up; and always as if their shape and colour were somehow already known to him; with the joy of recovery, as if his lighting upon them were a reassurance to him that he was in a world that was familiar. They were things he had been homesick for – that is what Adair felt. 'This,' he would say, waddling up to present them with a little marbled pebble. 'Pebble,' Virgilia would tell him. 'Yes,' he would say very solemnly, 'this.'

None of it was surprising to Adair, who had grown up with the belief, picked up from the girls in the kitchen, that he was a fairy child, who had to be humoured if he was not to forsake them and slip away. In fact he no longer believed that. It was just kitchen talk, old superstition. But some of the strangeness they had attributed to the child still lingered in the older boy's vision of him. That Fergus 'knew things' was only to be expected.

'Why,' Virgilia demanded. 'Why should he? What sort of things?'

Adair could not answer. 'You'll see,' he told her.

Meanwhile, just as she had done earlier with Adair, she taught the child to read. They began to take their lessons together, and afterwards, in the strange half-light of winter afternoons, would set off, Fergus dragging behind to peer at wonders they already knew, on expeditions into the abandoned rooms of the East Wing, where darker squares and rectangles on the faded wallpaper showed where landscapes and ghostly portraits had once shone. Dust lay thick on all the floors, cobwebs drooped from the ceiling and crammed the cupboards, which, when they tore the grey swags aside, revealed mops and buckets but also spinning wheels, a set of bowls that they sent cannoning into the walls, fishing-canes, great hooped skirts that the moths had reduced to bell-shapes of a dusty fabric you could poke a finger through, producing a trickle of grey mould that set them atchooing and blessing one another, portmanteaux and travelling-trunks from the Grand Tour, leather straps studded with horse-brasses, St Brighid's crosses. They wrote their names in the dust in their best copperplate, hauled out the trunks and found candlesticks and embroidered vestments in one, in another Alpine flowers and a little white bread-roll that looked fresh enough but had dried and was hard as stone.

They carried the fishing-canes down to the lake. The two boys took off their boots and stockings and waded in the slimy green water while fishlings in a burst of silver bubbles darted round their calves. Virgilia, bare-legged, with her skirt daintily lifted and a straw hat perched atop her curls, trailed through the shallows along the shore.

More and more they made up a company of their own. Isolated from all but their own interests, there grew up between them an intimacy of three that had its own changing history, its own moods and uneasy calms, its rivalries, struggles for supremacy, unstable resolutions. Its own language too, in which thoughts passed from one to another so easily that it scarcely mattered which of the three had given shape to a new thought or produced the code word that from now on would be a new element in their speech. A joke might be the beginning of it, or a new name for some object that had previously been designated by common syllables and only now revealed the special colour and glow that would make it part of their private world.

Virgilia remained the prime mover. Adair had long ago, and quite willingly, yielded authority to her. But Fergus, young as he was, could not so easily be controlled. He did not mean to deny her. It was simply that he had no idea what she wanted of him, it was not in his nature to be contained. When he fell into one of his freaks as she called it, she took it personally and protested, mildly at first. 'Fergus,' she would warn him, 'you're wool-gathering.' But he had no control over these moods. Almost unconscious of the extent to which he had moved away into a dimension of himself where he was absent in all but the flesh, he would, in a dreamy fashion, push her hand away. 'Leave me,' he would tell her. But she could not. When urgings and tugs failed to work she would begin to deliver little punches to his upper arm that became increasingly vehement, till he either came out of himself or ran away crying and calling her names learned from the stableboys that left her white-faced with affront.

Adair never felt closer to her than in these moments when all her attention was on Fergus and the whole of her intense being was set on breaking the boy, on winning him back. What touched him was the loss of all restraint in her, and when she was defeated, as she mostly was, the stricken look that drained her cheeks so completely of colour that you could see even the palest freckle on her skin, and under its fineness, a thing that never failed to astonish him, the blue, more intense than any sky-colour, of her veins. In being powerless she became transparent. What he loved in her, and all the more because she so rarely revealed it, was her vulnerability. It was here, he believed, that his advantage lay. She would see at last, she must, that her only peace, her only safety, was in him.

For by now they were no longer children.

There had been a time, not so long back, when she had suddenly leapt ahead of him. 'Don't,' she had told him when he tried to draw her into an old game of rough-and-tumble that would once have had her struggling fiercely beside them. He was hurt that if he touched her now she pulled away, offended that when he tried to force her she called him silly and stalked off.

'Oh leave her,' Fergus told him, 'if she doesn't want to play. We don't need *her*.' But it was no consolation to be paired in her eyes with a nine-year-old.

He stood and watched her go, no longer happy in the world Fergus offered but unable to follow. He could not grasp what had happened. Then the time came when he could and it was Fergus who was left. Almost from one day to the next they were in accord again, he and Virgilia, but in a way that was new and afforded him the keenest satisfaction, though there was a sense of mystery in it too that left him light-headed and even, at times, fearful; but it was a pleasurable fear.

Under the influence of all this he felt a new tenderness for himself. For his own body, first of all, its combination of strength and weakness, the uneasy power it contained, and at every moment of its contact with the world, its capacity for hurt; but then for the same quality, which seemed so obvious to him now, in others – Mama Aimée, Paddy, Virgilia. Most of all, Virgilia. Did she know how much she was at risk? He trembled when he thought of it. She was so reckless. Did she know how often she was playing in an area that neither of them had yet understood? In so much uncertainty, the one thing he knew for certain was that there had opened up around him, even as he began to feel his power, an immensity of the unknown, of what might never be known, that was a kind of terror to him, but to acknowledge the terror, he thought, was to get some measure of it and was a way to strength.

In the meantime the world had come alive for him with a new immediacy. He felt drugged at one moment with the drench and dazzle of things, and was charged the next with an energy that was not entirely his own.

One day when he had abandoned the others to be on his own, he found himself in the new oak-grove Eamon Fitz-gibbon had planted at the edge of the farm.

It was early spring. The young trees, which were as yet only twenty feet tall, were misted with green, but it was a greenness, as the pale sun caught it, that was more like a trick of the light than fleshy foliage.

What had carried him here, or so he had thought, was a mood, the need to catch up for a moment with his own tumultuous feelings. But when he stepped in among them he realized that the trees too were in a state of disturbance. Midges swarmed in their shade. The heat that had begun to gather, and which he felt as a dampness at the base of his spine, had set off an electric quivering in the air. It was, he saw now, the beginnings of a storm. How odd, he thought, when he looked up at the sky. There was no sign of a cloud there, only the spasms of a distant restlessness. Yet his body had felt the change, and in a moment he had confirmation of it from a different source.

In the crooked little avenues of an oak-trunk ants were swarming. They too had scented it. Some message had run from one to another of them, and now, in hundreds, which would soon be thousands, they were leaving their holes before the flood and excitedly climbing.

Looking in on their tiny lives, on bodies that in such a minute space could contain so much knowledge, will, all the co-ordination and discipline of an army, he had an apprehension of how crowded and complex his own body was, which did not seem at all lumpish or out of scale but on the contrary very finely adjusted, subtly attuned to everything that was happening here. The air crackled. All his senses were alert.

He should get out in the open, that is what he thought. No point in being struck. He plunged through bracken towards the open field, which was newly ploughed, the raw clods shining from the share, and there it was far off on the skyline, a cloud no bigger than his fist, but black as smoke and spreading, and above it lightning tremors, flash on flash.

He might have gone in then. There was still time to run for shelter. But he did not. He stood with his hands raised, rejoicing, when they came, in the first big splashes that wet his cheeks and darkened his shirt. Then, almost immediately, there was such a downrush of water that he might have been beaten flat into the earth. He was drenched – hair, clothes, skin – and staggering. The field turned to mud, then to liquid mud, he could barely keep upright in it. He heard his name called, and when he turned towards the source of it, saw emerging out of the thunderous light, as if it had somehow come to life from cold marble, what he took to be one of the statues in Eamon Fitzgibbon's gallery, a nereid that for a good while now he had guiltily stopped to contemplate and had gathered at last into the store of images he kept at the back of his head, her garments so liquefied and transparent that you saw through them the shape of her limbs and the small risen breasts, though the face was blunted and featureless like the face in a dream.

It was Virgilia, who had come out looking for him. She too was soaked, her garments liquefied, revealing the small risen breasts. She came up to him, laughing, reached for his hand, and clasped it as if she might otherwise have slipped and drowned. 'What are you doing?' she shouted.

He shook his head. For explanation he raised her hand and set it on his breast, as if it was there she would find her answer: in the flesh under his clinging shirt, in the clamouring of his heart. He felt freed by this new element they were in. To be drenched like this was a kind of nakedness. He lifted her hand to his mouth, as he never could have done if they had been in the presence of furniture. She did not object. When he lowered it, he let his head tilt forward and his lips found the softness of her neck. He was entirely without experience. Each of these actions was for itself. He did not think of them as leading anywhere.

The rain continued to hold them. As long as it lasted it was as if they had at last stepped outside the permitted and ordinary. But after a little her hand came up to his chest and pushed him off. He saw then that the rain was easing. They were in clear outline again and facing one another. But she was smiling.

They walked away hand in hand, slipping and sinking in the muddy furrows, hauling one another out. But what pleased her, he discovered after a time, was the belief that he had changed, had broken through into some part of himself where he was reckless. But it wasn't that. He had from beginning to end been following his body – that was all; doing what *it* wanted, what it told him to do. When he wandered away from them and sought the solitude of the oak-grove. When he stood waiting in the field for the rain to fall. When he called her to him and she had revealed herself and allowed him to touch her. She did not know it yet but he could do these things. This was just the beginning. He was patient. He would last.

In time Fergus too came into his growth. Too early, it seemed. He shot up so fast that there was half a year when he appeared to have outrun his strength. He had dizzy spells, all his clothes were too small for him, he had the awkward, unsteady look of a foal. At not quite thirteen, he was already a good head taller than either of them, with down on his lip and a new wildness in all his movements, though there were times still when he could be intimidatingly self-possessed. They felt he had not only caught up but surpassed them. Or the awakening, in his case, had been into a different order of beings. Of centaurs, Adair thought, since what the boy more and more resembled, with his long features and increasingly heavy limbs, was a kind of composite creature, half boy, half horse, as if Mama Aimée had found his image in a dream in which her passion for horses had worked deep in her womb to create this perfect union: a child so deeply attuned to the nature and being of horses that his body, at its time of change, had taken a unique course.

There was also the matter of his ghosts.

They had been taken often enough, on Sundays after Mass, to visit the little mounds at the end of the Walk, each stone with its familiar name and date; and Adair, who so far as he knew had no brother or sister of his own, had wondered what Fergus made of these small uninsistent sharers of his name. To be so singled out for survival, for life! To have put into your hands, and so firmly, the gift those others had let fall. Did this explain, perhaps, the sense he gave at times, and had always given, of being drawn away towards the margin of himself?

There was something else, Adair saw, that had shaped the boy, had shaped both of them.

Each Thursday now a dancing-master came to the Park to drill them in the niceties of the allemande and the quadrille. In one of those little insights his new self-consciousness afforded him he caught a vision of himself, of Fergus too, through the eyes of the slim-wristed straight-backed manikin with the fiddle tucked under his chin, who shook his head, cast his eyes up, and tapped with his bow for them to stop, go back to the spot he had marked on the floor and start again.

They were clodhoppers. That is what he saw. There was nothing in them of refinement or gentility. Their speech half the time was what they had picked up from Paddy and the grooms. They had none of the poise that had come to Virgilia as by second nature.

This had not concerned him till now because he had taken it as being required only of girls, of the sort of little lady Virgilia was bound to become because of the grandeur of the Park and the old-fashioned style that for all Eamon Fitzgibbon's Jacobin notions was preserved there. He saw now that the real cause was Ellersley, and though he burned with shame on his own part, he was also ashamed of what was revealed of the household, whose irregular life they had taken for granted, he and Fergus, and whose darker side was a secret that bound them in a silence they kept even with one another; but most of all, of what it revealed of the woman to whose kindness he owed his only place in the world.

He had always been fastidious. Now, at fifteen, he began to develop those habits of watchfulness and severe restraint that had always perhaps been the mark of his character but which the carelessness of life at Ellersley had obscured. He set himself apart from the disorder that surrounded him there, the crises, the scenes, but also, and painfully as the differences between them grew plainer, from Fergus.

As the little master of Ellersley Fergus was allowed to do pretty much as he pleased. In the early days he had often been as dirty when they set off for the Park as the children they passed on the way, who stood bare-legged and big-eyed to watch them go by in the cart, and he was not much less careless even now when it came to clean shirts and the dirt under his nails.

It was not in his nature to be resentful of the fact that Mama Aimée ignored and neglected him, and that his father, though he complained bitterly enough about how unruly the boy was, and what an impression he made of a half-tamed savage when he was dragged in to be shown off to company, did nothing to see that he was better looked after or in any way disciplined.

Mama Aimée, from being scared at first, in her super-stitious way, that if she showed too much affection for the child he would be snatched away, had drifted into a kind of indifference that was part habit and part a retreat from the world in general, for she had begun more and more these days to retire to her room, sometimes not emerging even for supper. It was also a response to Fergus himself, to some quality in him that scared her and which she did not want to face. She complained to Adair that she never saw the boy, that he deliberately avoided her, but the moment he appeared she was filled with a shrill impatience with everything he did, the way he walked and sat and stood, that puzzled Adair and left Fergus, who burned with shame to have the servants hear it, slack-shouldered and surly while she railed at him.

Adair too began to avoid her. She would waylay him on the stairs, a fearful apparition, since she only did it when she was in a 'condition'. Gaunt and grey, and half a head taller than he was, she would clasp him to her and weep. But he was no longer afraid of her outbursts, only embarrassed and obscurely ashamed. He knew now where the line lay between her emotions and his own.

'You avoid me,' she accused. 'You know how I need you, you're the only one now I can rely on, and you deliberately keep out of my way.'

'No,' he would say, shifting from foot to foot in an agony of distress.

'Look at me,' she would cry. 'Oh Michael, how can you be so cruel, how can you?'

'I don't mean to be cruel,' he would say, his lip trembling, and he would reach out and put his arms around her in the old way, but the fierceness with which she clung to him was frightful.

After a moment, abashed perhaps by a sudden sense of herself, she would release him, eyes closed, her hand patting at her unkempt hair. 'Where's Fergus?' she would ask, but in an abstracted way that worried and confused him. 'I never see him. Get him to come and see me – no, not now. In half an hour when I've had time to dress.'

She looked at Adair; reached out, touched his face.

'Poor Michael,' she said tenderly, 'I'm so sorry! I shouldn't do this to you. But you'll forgive me, I know you will.'

He stood shaking his head. He was trying not to let her see how he pitied her, but how unnerved he was too by the disorder she represented, the pressure she put upon him. She was always trying to enlist him in some conspiracy against Fergus, whom she accused now of deliberately thwarting her, of trying to humiliate her in front of the neighbours and put her in the wrong with his father.

In fact none of this was true. Fergus acted only to suit himself. Selfishly perhaps, but innocently. He was entirely without guile. But when Adair told her this she was furious.

'You're like all the rest – Paddy, all of them – you take his part against me. He pulls the wool over your eyes just as he does the others – you most of all, because he knows you will never think ill of him. He's a demon. He isn't my child, I've always known that. He was sent to torment me. – No Michael, don't go, don't turn away.'

'My mother's mad, don't you know that?'

Adair was shocked by the matter-of-factness with which Fergus could say this, the detachment it suggested in one so young. He was twelve years old.

'It's a shame and I'm sorry, but I don't mind it so much. I don't like to see her, that's all. I'm sorry for her, but I don't want to see her. You should keep away from her too, Mickey.'

Their eyes met and it was Adair who first dropped his gaze.

'But it's all right,' he added after a moment, 'if you feel you can't. I know she depends on you, and I know you don't take sides against me.'

Occasionally, when she was in one of her sociable phases, she would invite some of the better class of neighbours, in the hope that he and Fergus might make friends among the children and get invited to dances and Christmas parties. They went into Oughterard to be measured by Mr Flynn the tailor. She ordered patent-leather dancing-pumps and smart waistcoats and gloves to make them presentable, and the sitting-room was cleared of its furniture and rugs and little gilt-legged chairs were arranged around the walls. Preparations were made in the kitchen for a buffet of pies and sweet jellies and cakes.

But they were painful occasions. Mama Aimée, though she behaved with unfailing courtesy even to the most tiresome of her guests, was in a highly nervous state, afraid that the band she had hired, which consisted of fiddlers who were more often to be heard at county fairs, would play badly and that the more fashionable young people would reject the flavours Mrs Upshaw had decided on for the jellies; or that their two footmen, who were raw and inexperienced youths, would not show to advantage in their livery. When the younger boys went sliding over the floor in improvised races, she got flustered and did not know whether to intervene or simply let them be. Only when the whole company had taken the floor in a mazurka or quadrille did she feel quite safe and settle sufficiently to enjoy the colour, the music, the fresh faces, and the ease with which Fergus, in spite of his coltish six-feet, which made him tower over the other children his age, performed his *chassés en avant*, *chassés en arrière* and *glissade* as the dancing-master had taught them.

He was wonderfully high-spirited and made a great

impression, even on the grown-ups. But there it ended. The boys of his own age were scared by his wildness, and the girls, who were attracted by it, even some of the older ones, who had heard of it from their brothers, did not interest him.

'I'm ashamed of you,' Mama Aimée told him bitterly when the coats and shawls and overshoes had been redeemed from the cloakroom Paddy had organized at the bottom of the stairs and the noise of farewells had quietened, the last carriages rolled off, and they were settled for a moment in the first-floor sitting-room. 'I doubt the McCafferties will come here again, you were so rude to them.'

Fergus, still flushed and excited, was sprawled on a sofa, his long legs thrust out before him.

She regarded him over the rim of her teacup. Everything about him, Adair saw, was unacceptable to her. But why? The glow of sweat on his downy upper lip, his hair, which was damp and had come loose from its knot, his big hands, the space he took up with his long legs. It was as if the glow he gave off was a personal affront to her, the release of so much hot energy into the world, so much untameable will, an indiscretion on her part for which she could not forgive herself.

The boy felt her displeasure and waited, tense, undefiant, for the storm to break. But for once she could find no particular on which to attack him. Frowning, she rose, set her cup down, and stalked off. A little smile of satisfaction came to his lips as he watched her go.

But a moment later he sank deeper into the sofa, thrust his legs out further across the gleaming parquet, and covered his eyes.

They did not make friends among the local families. They did get invited to parties and dances but as often as not failed to go, either because they had grown out of last year's jacket or dancing-shoes and Mama Aimée had neglected to order new ones, or because at the last moment the carriage was not ready, or she was out of sorts and there was no one else to send with them; or because she had seen, Adair suspected, that Fergus wanted to go and had manufactured these excuses to prevent it. Fergus did not complain of these minor persecutions any more than he had complained earlier of her neglect, and put on such a show of easy indifference that even Virgilia, who was sharp, did not see how he had been hurt.

It was at this time that Adair began to see that Virgilia's feeling for Fergus was no longer one of those shifting and inconsequential alliances, based on a word or a whim or the many little dissatisfactions and bursts of sympathy that till now had characterized the movement of emotion between them.

One afternoon, he and Fergus had been playing shuttle-cock while Virgilia, book in hand, looked on. They had taken their shirts off in the heat, and when the game was over, used them to dry off. Stretched out beside her in the grass, which was cooling on the skin, they slept.

Waking, he looked up from where he had thrown his forearm across his eyes to keep off the sun.

Virgilia, her knees drawn up under her skirt, had laid her book aside and was staring with a dreamlike fixity at the muscles of Fergus's throat, which tensed, went lax, then tensed again, as with his limbs flung out and his bare chest lightly heaving, he slept. Her lips were parted. Her teeth glistened. She looked, Adair thought, as if she were drugged.

Desire, that is what he saw. But also that desire was a part of her nature. He had consoled himself till now with the belief that it was not, or that she had not yet discovered it; and for no other reason than that he desired her and she had shown no response.

As for Fergus, he seemed entirely unaware. He watched him, watched them both – he had discovered a new talent in himself, though he took no pride in it, that of the spy; but was convinced after a time that his first impression was a right one. Fergus knew nothing of the change in Virgilia's feelings. Adair was angry with him now on new grounds. For the innocence, the indifference it might be, that allowed him to hurt her and remain blithely unconscious of it.

He kept all this to himself, and it was typical of Fergus, he thought, when the boy at last challenged him, that he should be so sensitive to his feelings when he was so oblivious to hers.

'What is it, Mickey?' he demanded in his forthright way. 'You're angry with me, I know you are. But why? What have I done?'

'I'm not angry,' Adair told him.

Fergus turned away.

'Now,' Adair said, 'you are angry with me.'

'Yes I am, of course I am. Because you feel something and you deny it. Why should you lie? Is it Virgilia?'

'Perhaps.'

'You don't have to fear that, Mickey. I know what you feel for her. Do you think I would do anything to hurt you?'

'No, I know you wouldn't. But you hurt her.'

'Virgilia? What do you mean? How do I hurt her? I'm the same as I ever was.'

'But she is not.'

Fergus looked away and shook his head.

They were making their way to the Park across-country, through a patch of dank wood thick with sycamore and whitethorn that freighted the air with its suffocating sweetness, and foxgloves in purple clumps. In spring you could find Irish orchids here, if you knew where to look, and in autumn mushrooms. But now it was June. The air was hot and close. They sweated, their shirts sticking to their backs and the flies swarming.

They came out into waist-high meadowsweet and Fergus strode ahead, slashing at the flowerheads left and right with a hazel-switch. There was nothing more he would say. He would, as he always did, take this into himself, but they would not speak of it again.

Adair had always understood that the position he occupied in Mama Aimée's household, however completely he was accepted and however fond they might be of him, made his prospects very different from those that Fergus could look forward to. One day he would have to leave the security of Ellersley and strike out on his own. That was the way his future lay. He had always known this and had thought Fergus knew it too, though they had never discussed the thing. Now, at nearly seventeen, he thought they must.

'What do you mean?' Fergus demanded. 'What are you telling me?'

They were camping out, as they often did on early summer nights, on the slopes of Ben Breen. A fire of twigs and heather made a blaze between stones.

They had ridden up here through fields of bog-asphodel with their spires of star-shaped, spiky blossom, past flocks of sheep that wandered the unenclosed uplands, leaving the gorse hung with wisps of dirty wool like old man's beard. Their horses, pale shadows in the moonlight, were set loose now, cropping the short grass between sheets of stone. They lifted their heads as if they smelled something, a ghost or the scent on the air of a fox. 'Shh there,' Fergus whispered, and at the sound of his voice they settled. In the easy intimacy of the moment Adair had spoken out.

'I mean,' he said, trying to make it sound undramatic – he was shocked by the violence of Fergus's response – 'that I may have to go away very soon now. I can't live off Mama Aimée all my life. I have to make my own way in the world. You will inherit Ellersley – '

'And you think I'd send you away?'

The boy's honour was touched, or some fear, which hurt him, that Adair might doubt his affection. He was at an age of half-childhood, half-manhood where everything stirred him. The tautness of his shoulders in the firelight made him seem painfully thin.

'I know you wouldn't, I don't say that. But my life is to be different from yours. My circumstances are different – don't you know that?' He threw a fistful of twigs into the fire and they caught and crackled into flame. The heat that hit his face hid the emotion he felt. 'I don't mean tomorrow, but one day, in a little time now, I must go. And because I know I must I have begun to look forward to it.'

Fergus gave him a hard look, then frowned and turned away.

Adair was surprised. Didn't he know all this? In the close sharing of so much that was secret but silent between them hadn't the boy understood that what made life so hard for him, his uneasy place in the world, could not be changed by affection, even *his* affection, or the avowal that he would never be anything less than a dear older brother and the one person in the world he could not do without.

He saw how distressed Fergus was and was sorry. He hated to see him hurt. Most of all, he thought, it was a kind of shame; at having failed to see what ought to have been obvious, and for the doubt it might cast on the depth of his nature or his love.

'But it's not right,' he said simply.

'It's the way it is,' Adair told him. 'It's no fault of yours – or mine either. It's the way the world is.'

'I'd have made the world very different, if I'd had the making of it. I'll give you half of whatever it is – all if you'll take it. Then you can stay.'

'You would, I know you would, but my life is – Every man's life is his own, that's what I believe – Kismet. I have to make what I can of it. And you know, it isn't as easy as that, you can't just give things away.'

'Why can't I?'

'Because that's the life *you've* been given.'

'I'm not free – is that what you mean? We're not free.' He shook his head. 'That's not what Eamon Fitzgibbon tells us.'

'No, it's not. But I'm not sure I believe him. Anyway, you couldn't because it's not the way things are done.'

'Then we should change them. Shouldn't we?'

'You would,' he said affectionately, and it was true. He would. That was his style.

'What you really mean is you wouldn't accept.'

'That too, I couldn't. Not because I think you wouldn't do it gladly, I know you would, but because it's already settled in my mind. I mean to hire myself out as a soldier. That's the honourable Irish thing to do.'

'Then I'll go with you.'

He must have caught, Adair thought, the little movement with which he looked away.

'Do you really think,' he flashed out, 'that I mean to stay here and sit playing whist all night, and starve my tenants, and be a fat do-nothing like my father – '

'You shouldn't speak like that of – '

'Shouldn't? Why is it always should and shouldn't with you, Mickey? I don't think that way. Neither does Virgilia.'

The barb shot home. Adair winced but would not let it pass.

'Because you do not have to, you and Virgilia. I do. It's what I've been trying to make you see. Our circumstances' – he went back to the word because he found a kind of pleasure in its cruel objectivity – 'are different. It doesn't mean we are not close, and fond of one another. We are, you know it. But I have to think about such things. Or it's my nature – I suppose it is.'

Suddenly Fergus burst into tears.

'I don't know why you are saying these things,' he said fiercely. Adair was shocked. He hadn't expected this.

Fergus got up and crossed quickly to where his horse stood and put his arms around the big bay's neck.

It was a moment Adair would return to again and again, looking up through the waves of heat from the fire to the quivering image that haunted him still of Fergus, his arms round the horse's neck, leaning his brow for comfort against the huge shadowy creature that turned its head in sympathy and tried to nuzzle his cheek.

But his own heart for the moment was hardened. Let him accept the conditions of his life, he thought. I have accepted mine.

There was an element of deliberate cruelty in it, that was the reflection, he saw, of a bitterness in him that he had failed, for all his philosophy, to suppress. But it was not Fergus he had meant to punish.

The image burned in him still, and clearer now for having been sharpened in memory by the times he had gone back to conjure it; no longer with the heat of the fire to make it shift and waver in the light, so that boy and horse, all airy illusion, might have been suspended a foot above the earth, but grounded at last in a real weight of bone, and in a sorrow he felt with all the heaviness of his regret that the moment should stand so clearly as the end of something. Do not turn, he found himself saying, as if he could arrest the moment and stop time from moving on.

But the boy had turned, calm again, and walked slowly to the fire, and sat, and something new had begun between them.

He held on now to the old image, boy and horse; held it clear in his mind, let all the rush of feeling that swelled his heart touch it with a light that made the whole hut blaze up so that even Daniel Carney must be aware of it, and put the question that was meant to lead Carney to his own version of it – Fergus, taller now, broader, a dozen years older, and the horse no longer the bay, Eldrich, but a black Arabian brought in via India. If he could only see clearly enough what Daniel Carney conjured up and made burn in the dark between them, he might have something like proof.

So once again, but beginning some way off so that the man himself would find his way to it, he spoke.

5

'TELL ME SOMETHING,' Adair said, subdued, matter-of-fact, 'about your time out there on the ranges.'

Carney looked up. His face brightened.

'Ah,' he said, 'that was a grand time. I niver in all me days knew a better.'

'Wasn't it hard? To be in hiding always, on the run. I've seen the place. It's rough country.'

'It is, sir, it is rough. It amazed me sometimes – you know, the horses. How they could manage it. They're amazing creatures, don't you think, sir, the way they adapt? But a hard life is what I've always had, it wasn't no harder than the rest. An' for the first time, like, I had companions.' He mused on this and slowly shook his head. 'No, it wasn't hard, even the sleepin' rough with not a bit of a shed or that to crawl into when the rain come peltin'. At least there was no mortar to pound or rocks to break and no man standin' over you.'

'And the others? Were they runaways too?'

'One was, Lonergan, the others wasn't. Cassidy, for instance. Well, I reckon he must a' been runnin' from something, he was the sort nothin' can hold. You know, wild, he was as wild a feller as I ever come across. But nobody was after him. He just rode up one day out of nowhere and says, "I'm Cassidy," and that was that.' He gave a throaty laugh. 'The troopers couldn' find us, but he did. Rode right up out of nowhere an' announced himself, "I'm Cassidy," just like that, an' there he was, told us 'e was sixteen. We believed it at first, 'e was tall enough. Skinny as a broomstick but tall. It was on'y later we found out different. And fierce. If he thought you were makin' fun of 'im he'd get that mad you had to worry he might just up an' put a bullet between your eyes. He was capable of it, he'd of done it sure as winkin'. Knew more 'n a hundred songs I reckon, words 'n all. 'E weren't much of a singer, for the voice like, but 'e'd picked up all the words somehow and wasn't shy about beltin' out a tune.' He shook his head. 'I'm sorry they got 'im.'

'They say he shot two men who weren't even armed. Made them kneel down in a barn and put a bullet into the back of their neck.'

'I can believe that. It's what I said, he was fierce. Considerin'.'

'Considering his age, you mean?'

'Yes, sir, that too. I don't know, just considerin'.' He sat silent a moment. 'He was always itchin' to do something – we weren't active enough for 'im. He couldn' sit still, even for a minute, and we did a lot of, you know, just sittin' around an' waiting, sittin' the days out. Wet days, days when we had to stay put, lie low, like. Dolan was always very cautious. I reckon' ol' Luke was disappointed in us. There'd been – you know, a lot of talk in the towns about what a dangerous lot we was, and he'd heard it. He was expectin' more. We weren't wild enough for 'im.' He laughed outright.

'What were you waiting for, that Dolan had to be so – cautious?'

'For our tracks to go cold. If we'd slipped into some little settlement and, like, done something.'

'Is that all?'

98

'What do you mean?'

'Wasn't he maybe waiting for something else?'

'Like what, sir?'

'For someone to contact him. Some group, for instance.'

'Oh,' the man said, 'the Irish, you mean. That was just talk. There wasn't no gathering intended, if that's what you mean.'

'Are you sure?'

The man looked at him hard. A small line of self-assertion came to the broken face. 'I was there,' he said. 'Wouldn' I know if there was something like that goin'?'

'Not if he didn't mean you to,' Adair said coolly.

Carney frowned and dropped his head. When he glanced up again the eyes had a sidelong, injured look. 'Why shouldn't he?' he said at last. 'I was one of 'em. We was all in it together.'

'Maybe he didn't want too many of you to be in the know.'

'You mean in case we got caught?'

'That would be one reason.'

The man shook his head rapidly from side to side. He was beginning to be distressed. 'You're wrong, sir. You don't understand. There wasn't a man of us would have given 'im away. Not for any money,' he said passionately. 'Not for our lives.'

Adair let a little time pass – Carney, meanwhile, continued to sit tense and troubled – then he said: 'You weren't with him from the beginning.'

'No, I wasn't, it's true. But I was there at the end. An' if there was anything like that intended I would of known. Rebellion is a serious thing. Even I know that. We would of known. He would of told us.'

'But you were rebels already, weren't you?'

'I was a runaway, sir. Maybe that made me a rebel, I don't know. Is that what they say? Am I to be hanged as a rebel?'

Adair shook his head. 'No,' he said, 'there'll be no talk of rebellion. But would you care so much?'

'No, sir, it'd be all the same to me. It'll be all the same, as far as I'm concerned, this time tomorrer. It's just that it wasn't so. I was there. I know what it was.'

'So who was with him,' Adair persisted, 'before you?'

'Lonergan. McBride – '

'Wasn't McBride the first?'

'Yes sir, you're right in that, he was. I think 'e was. They'd bin together a few months. Up north somewhere.'

'And suppose I told you McBride was also a runaway – '

'He wasn't, sir. I'd of known if 'e was – '

'Not your ordinary sort of convict. A political. And that he was in contact with others, an Irish group up at Castle Hill. Did you ever hear any talk of that? Or see any letters?'

'I told you already, sir, I can't read.'

'I mean, did you see any brought? To McBride. Or Dolan. Or carried away again?'

Carney shook his head. He looked desperately unhappy. Adair feared he might at any moment cut the conversation off and turn away. It was shameful, he knew, to harry the man like this, to unsteady his last hour or two with useless doubts.

He had no interest in the official rigmarole of unrest and rebellion; not much belief in it either. Though he could not be sure of this, he was inclined to set it down to the large measure of fantasy that governed what happened here, in a place where rumour – the insignificant dust-whirl, not much bigger than your hand, that in just minutes could build,

100

circle on circle, into a raging vortex – too easily replaced reasonable argument. But somewhere, somewhere in all this, if he drove the man hard enough, was the breakaway word, the one identifying fact, that would bring him certainty. At the expense – he knew he could in no way justify the exaction – of this poor fellow's distress.

'Could it be,' he said at last, 'that Cassidy didn't just find you, as you say, but knew where to come because he was sent?'

'But 'e was just a kid. He never knew any more about such things than I did, than any of us did. You're mistaken, sir, I know you are. All he ever talked about was – you know, women an' that. What'd 'e'd done in this place, what 'e'd got up to in that. But to tell the truth, no one of us ever believed 'e'd 'ad more than a sniff of a cunt – I'm sorry, sir. It got on our nerves sometimes, the way 'e went on about it. I don't know, sir, I don't know –' He was terribly agitated, trying to hang on hard to his view of what had happened, the way things had been. 'I think you must be wrong, sir. It wasn't the way you're suggestin'. I know it wasn't, I was there.'

'All right, all right, Carney, don't distress yourself, we'll drop it. It doesn't matter at this date.'

'You're right, sir, it doesn't. They're all dead anyway, God help 'em.'

'It's all right. No need to say any more of it.'

Carney sat hunched into himself. He was silently shaking his head. 'You mustn' ask me any more questions, sir, I won't answer 'em. I won't say any word more of it.' He shook his head again, and said, as if to himself: 'It'll be over soon enough.'

'I was just going to ask about something else. Don't worry, it's not about that business. I was going to ask about

101

the songs Cassidy sang. You said he knew a lot of songs. There's no harm in that, is there?'

'No, sir, I suppose there isn't. They was comic mostly, we got a good laugh out of 'em. Bawdy. Do you know that word, sir? Is it right? Bad, like. But he could do all the voices and make you laugh.'

'Are they the ones Dolan liked?'

'They were, yes. He was like the rest of us in that. He liked a good laugh.'

'And there were sad ones as well? Irish songs?'

'Yes. A few, not so many. I'm gettin' a bit tired now, sir, if you don't mind. I reckon I might try to sleep.'

'Was there one that was a favourite with him?'

'With Cassidy, sir?'

'With all of you. Dolan, for instance.'

'Yes, there might of been.'

'Can you remember what it was?'

'Not the words, sir. I'm no good for words.'

'The tune, then.'

'Do you mean can I sing it?'

'Yes. It might settle us. Then we could try to sleep.'

'Well then – '

He began to croon an old air that was familiar enough but was not, as Adair had hoped it might be, one of the songs they had learned in the kitchen at Ellersley or sung on more formal occasions in the music room at the Park. The man's voice was rough, and shaky at first, but he held a tune well, and as he warmed to it there was, in the close dark of the hut, a sadness, a kind of beauty too, in the way the melody rose and was held a moment, a long high moment, on the man's breath, prolonged in the exaggerated Irish fashion, Adair thought, that had a natural theatricality and sense of performance to it.

The shape it made created its own following silence, and they sat, both, in the ease of it. Once again they were, as the old tune lingered, just two men in the one place, in the one moment together, and far from where they had begun.

'I think I'll just sleep a little,' Carney said. He rolled himself in his blanket, turned away, and must have dropped off almost immediately.

Alone again in the half dark and listening to his laboured breathing, Adair felt a kind of desolation creep over him. The edges of his being grew fuzzy, acquired the unreality of a dream – and not his own dream either. He might have been conjured up, he felt, out of the other's uneasy sleep, and left dangling, with no will or purpose of his own, till the man's consciousness, here in these last hours of a life about which he knew nothing except the official facts, discovered a reason for his presence and devised a form, however irrational, that would allow him to act and speak.

So he thought, and only after a good deal of time had passed, in which he was blown upon the air, disembodied, aimless, did he understand that this was his own dream. He was sleeping, but lightly enough to have taken the other's breathing, which he was still aware of, for his own, as if Carney had taken on the job of drawing breath for both of them, so that when the man spoke he was startled, had to catch back, he felt, the responsibility of breathing for himself, an old habit that for a space he had been in danger of losing.

'I'm sorry, sir, were you sleeping? I've got a gut-ache. It comes on sudden, like. I need to use the bucket.'

It took Adair a moment to grasp what he meant.

'I'm sorry, sir. If you was sleepin'.'

'No,' Adair said. 'No. It's early yet. I could do with stretching my legs for a bit.'

He got to his feet, rather stiffly, and pushed at the door, letting in a flood of moonlight. The fuzziness he had felt sprang into focus. Air, a breath of pine. Heavy. Resinous. He was himself again.

6

STEPPING OUT INTO the chill of it, Adair was struck once again by the vastness of the world up here on the high plains, by how much closer the sky was – so close you felt the weight of the stars, their mineral quality, and marvelled that they should hang there, glowing and turning.

The earth was all dazzle. Smoky shadows flowed across it and seemed, in their blue-blackness, more substantial than what cast them, a line of clouds just lit at the edge by a risen but invisible moon. Other shadows were on the move among the she-oaks that marked the edge of the stream. These were the horses, his own chestnut among them, and it was she, sensing his presence, who made a movement more nervous than hitherto and set the little mob going at a more rapid pace, back and forth, unsettling the dark.

After the hut, with its close smell of humanity and its earthy damp, the sharpness in his nostrils made him dizzy. That or his empty stomach. I'll eat something now, he thought. But before he approached the fire with its companionable glow, he lifted his face once again to the vastness of the night.

Sometimes, when the moon was just a sliver, the fact of its being reversed down here gave you the odd sensation of being turned about, as if you had somehow got yourself on the wrong side of the mirror. He was used to working by the sky. As a boy, walking back at night from the Park, and later bivouacked on the Polish plain, he had found a kind of assurance in the stars up there being so punctual as they rolled towards dawn, and in knowing, because Eamon Fitzgibbon had taught them to him, the names like old friends of the various constellations, all drawn as they were out of folk-tales or classical mythology, Charles's Wain, the Pleiades, Berenice's Hair.

Here there was a different sky to read. He had had to begin all over again, as if he had been set down on a new planet rather than the far side of the old one. He let the cold air fill his lungs now and resettled himself by naming, and allowing to blaze out in his head, the bright star up there in the very centre of the heavens, Canopus, like the point of a tent-pole from which the whole blazing firmament was suspended; for a moment he felt closer to it, far off as it was, than to the fire not twenty yards off with its promise of food and talk.

Suddenly, all in a rush and at a speed he might have thought unnatural, the moon sailed out. The horses now were a play of luminous forms among the trees, dilating and darkening, massing, then breaking, and lit from behind by the firelight flames, and all at different angles, the men's heads turned towards him. A fair boy leapt to his feet.

'I thought,' Adair said, 'I might get a bite to eat.'

He moved to join them.

'Stew,' the boy offered. 'There's Kersey's stew.'

'You'll be sorry,' said another youth, who sat up from where he had been laid out with his head against his pack-saddle.

'Don't you take no notice of 'em,' Kersey put in, making a place for him. 'They talk like that just for the sake of it. It's pigeon, topknots. I shot 'em meself. An' a couple a' bronzewings. It's good.'

'I'll make some tea to wash it down,' the fair boy, Langhurst, offered. He took up a sooty quart-pot. 'We'll need more wood,' he said significantly, setting off for the creek, and the other, the lean dark one, shifted his haunches, rose up and followed. Adair heard the horses stir as Langhurst approached them, then his voice where he had stopped a moment to settle them. It travelled so clearly on the still air that he might have been back again at their side.

They are all very accommodating, he thought, these fellows. Even the black had stirred at his presence. But only to the extent, he saw, of moving further into the shadows on the far side of the fire, where, cross-legged and guardedly intent, he could make himself invisible, Adair thought, to whatever authority he might represent.

Kersey meanwhile, from a billy on the fire, ladled a mound of thick stew on to a plate and handed him a wooden spoon. Then stood waiting for him to taste it and approve.

He took a good spoonful and looked up, nodding. It was too hot in his mouth to allow of speech. Kersey, appeased or justified, went back to lying with one knee crooked upon the other, a begrimed and bony foot dangling in the air and swinging.

'It's good,' Adair said at last. It was, too.

'Them boys complain just for the sake of it,' Kersey told him again. 'Just t' hear themselves speak. I don't take no notice of it.'

Langhurst, looming up out of the dark, heard him and gave a derisive chuckle. He squatted and settled the pot over the fire.

'He ain't the worst of 'em,' Kersey said.

'I suppose that's me, is it?' said the lean boy, Garrety, who appeared with a pile of branches in his arms, which he dumped unceremoniously beside the fire. In the sudden updraught the fire snapped, then flared, sending up a shower of sparks, a dozen of which caught Langhurst's sleeve where he was still squatting.

'Hey,' he shouted, leaping up and beating at his jacket. 'Watch what you're doing, you silly bugger. You almost set fire to me.'

'Oh, stop moanin',' the other retorted, mock-weary. 'You ain't hurt. The tea ain't spilled, is it?'

'They're like an old married couple,' Kersey told him confidentially. 'They never let up. Scrap like that night an' noon.'

'Shut yer mouth, Kersey,' the lean boy said, but mildly. 'No one ast your opinion.'

They went on like this, cheerfully trading insults, and Adair had the sense of its being a show put on especially for him, to demonstrate how lively and aggressive they were, its form so settled as to be merely ritual.

He was not ready for this sort of banter. Some part of him was still delayed in the hut. And his arrival, he saw, put a kind of restraint upon them, for all their attempt at lightness. It wasn't simply the difference in rank, or the fact that he was new and made them self-conscious of habits that had grown up between them that a stranger might find dubious. Kersey, he guessed, had already brought them news that he was ill-humoured and hard to please.

The pannikins of sweet tea helped. Langhurst poured and handed them round, after he had risen up and swung the billy three times overarm to settle the leaves. They sat quietly sipping. After a little, in quite a different mood, as if, after the explosive activity around his arrival, they had moved back to some previous moment, Langhurst, with a half-apologetic glance in his direction, enquired of the other, 'So go on, Garrety, what happened then? What'd you do?'

There was in his voice none of its earlier harshness, which even then Adair had thought forced. Its quality now was of an almost childlike openness, which was all it needed to change the mood of the group, to make it seem, as the night closed round them, close-bound in stillness and expectancy. They had, after their interval of rough play and manly belligerence, reverted to story-telling, these youths, and with that to some more contemplative version of themselves that depended, Adair thought, on these ancient conditions of deep night and a fire kept burning to lead a man's suspended self into the breathing heart of things.

'Go on, Garrety,' Langhurst insisted, 'finish it.'

Garrety suppressed a smile. All cheekbones and narrow jaw, he had a face that might have been vicious. The sockets of his eyes were dark, with a fiery point in each, reflections of the fire or some other flame. He moved away into himself before he answered, in a way that seemed unlikely in the truculent fellow of just moments ago. It's an act, Adair thought. This fellow's a satirist.

'So I said to 'im, what d'you want, Jacko, why me?'

He might have been speaking from a stage. His voice had a dramatic ring to it, leapt past them and seemed projected towards a figure who had stepped out of the night to join them. Langhurst cast a glance over his shoulder, then, with a child's delighted readiness to be harrowed, turned back, grinning.

'He laughed then, that was the odd thing. After all that, he laughed. You'd of expected a ghost to be, you know, solemn – mournful. But he laughed in an easy way, as if 'e knew something I didn't.' He frowned. 'I wanted to turn me back then and just walk away, on'y I couldn't. I felt like he was holding me there. I mean, like *he* was the one seeing *me*, rather than the other way round, an' I couldn't go till he decided to stop and let me, I was too – light, that's what I felt. And the fact is, I wasn't the one he was after, it wasn't me, I never done it. I told 'im that. I told him: it wasn't me, mate, I never done it, you've got this all arse up. He put a smirk on 'is face at that and just looked at me as if he knew better. I was surprised. I always thought – you know, that once you were passed over you'd know everything at last, all the answers, that's what I would of expected.'

'Yes,' Langhurst said dreamily, 'me too. That's what I would of thought too.'

'Well, he didn't. That must've been why he was hangin' about. To find out. Anyway, after a bit the weight sort of come back to me, I could move. Then 'e was gone.'

Langhurst waited. The story-teller had gone sombre. Maybe he isn't a satirist after all, Adair thought. The skin was tight over his cheekbones, the eyes narrowed.

'And was that the end of it?'

'Yair, well, I never saw no more of 'im, if that's what you mean. On'y I couldn't fathom why he thought it was me that done it. I didn't, I never would have. But he thought I would and that worried me. I felt – you know, that he knew something I didn't. About me, I mean. Anyway, after a bit, when he didn' come back, I reckoned, he's found out who it really was. You see, he'd been after all of us, one by one, till he found out.'

'And who was it?' Langhurst asked, as if this story like all others must have a satisfactory end.

'Hell, I don't know. It wasn't me, that's all I know.'

'Did the others tell you anything?'

'No, an' I didn' ask 'em neither, I didn' want to know. It wasn't my life. On'y, about a year later, another one of 'em, Brat Crawley, got drowned in a flash flood up Richmond way, that just sort of rose up out of nowhere. One minute he was there, the next he wasn't. Gone. Swept right off 'is feet.'

'Were you there? Did you see it?'

'Nah. Heard about it. Another feller, Lucky, he saw it. He

110

was right behind 'im, ready t' lead his horse down the bank. Bam!'

Langhurst waited. 'An' you reckon it might have been him?' he said at last. 'This Brat – what's-'is-name?'

'Crawley. Brat Crawley.' Another ghost, in fierce affront at this suggestion, might have risen up and been standing where Garrety stared away past the fire.

'I didn't say that. No, I wouldn't reckon so. It was just a coincidence. It didn't necessarily mean nothin'. Just a lot of weird circumstances, one after the other.'

Langhurst seemed impressed. In the quietness that fell the two youths, who all this time had been speaking as if they were alone here, so rapt were they by some concern of their own, sat stilled, each with his own preoccupations. Kersey too was stilled. The black, Jonas, who throughout had sat deeply enthralled, hanging with drawn breath on the line of Garrety's voice but attending to the hushed mood of the telling, Adair thought, rather than to its words or events, had gone most still of all. It was the intensity he established there, as of a darkness more dense, more tautly gathered, that drew Adair's gaze.

He was a scrawny fellow who might have been sixteen but could also have been forty. The wear and tear his body had taken was not measurable in white man's years.

He wore the jacket and trousers of a trooper, but the trousers were too short above his lean shanks and the jacket so frayed at the elbows and cuffs that the thin threads had lost all colour. He had not solved as yet, either at chest or flies, the relationship of buttonholes to buttons.

The uniform was an irrelevance – that's what you felt. Like another form of body decoration, it was no more than the sign, loosely assumed, that he had been brought over from savagery into the service of a remote and ineffectual authority. His nakedness was still intact.

He was, Adair thought, even under his name of Jonas, an opening there into a deeper darkness, into a mystery – of the place, of something else too that was *not-place*, which might also be worth exploring – but all traffic through it, in either direction, was blocked.

Suddenly there was a sound off in the night. It had the clarity and sharpness of a shot and seemed unnervingly close.

'What was that?' Langhurst whispered.

Kersey laughed.

'A fish,' he said, 'a fish jumpin'.'

'Didn't sound like a fish.'

'Did to me. Creek's full of 'em. I'll be after one or two of them in the mornin' for our breakfast. Perch. What'd you think it was, I wonder?' He chuckled and turned to Adair. 'Fish,' he said again, inclined to pursue this small advantage at the younger trooper's expense. Langhurst ignored him.

'Well,' he said, harking back to what Garrety had been telling, 'I never experienced nothing like that.'

He said this ruefully, out of a sense, Adair felt, of inveterate youthfulness, as if he had missed out on something, but there was as well a note of apprehension in his voice, as if it might be an experience, one of many, that was still to come and he was uncertain till it did how he would meet it.

Garrety broke out of his stillness. With his heel he kicked reflectively at the sandy earth.

'You seem to know an awful lot a fellers,' Kersey put in, 'that come to a bad end. Better watch out, Ben. One day yer mate here'll be tellin' the same sort o' story about you.'

'What's that supposed to mean?'

It was Langhurst again, his tone one of aggrieved offence on the part of his friend.

'Oh, nothin',' Kersey told him wearily. 'Don't bother about me.'

'We don't,' Langhurst shot back. 'On'y don't bother to put your oar in if you got nothing to say.' He turned again to Garrety, afraid these interruptions might have broken the other's mood.

'So then – you said *twice*. What was the other one?'

'It wasn't a person,' Garrety said.

Langhurst leaned forward, waited.

'What then?'

'A kind of – event.'

'Go on.'

But Garrety now seemed unwilling to be drawn, to evoke, even for himself, whatever it was that haunted him. He looked haunted.

'I don't know what it was really,' he said. 'I was crossin' this big paddock out Camden way. It was a place I knew well enough, I'd been there often enough. I was just walkin' across it. 'Bout four in the afternoon. I wasn't in a hurry. But somethin' – I don't know what – must of stopped me. I just stood there, I don't know how long, but it seemed long. I felt something strange was happening. Not to me but all round me. Like a wind had come up. Only it wasn't that. The air was still, stiller than it had been, in fact – no birds, no crickets. That's odd, I thought. I could hear the grass-blades rubbing one against the other, a weird sound, that once you noticed it got louder and louder, like someone was going at a knife-blade with a stone – you know what that sounds like. Only loud. As if it was hundreds of 'em. Something made me look down then. I was standin' in blood. It was all around me, filling the whole paddock like a lake, I was up to me ankles in it! I smelt it then, and felt

113

its wetness, the air was so thick I could hardly breathe. An' all of a sudden there were these voices, cryin' out something terrible, I never heard nothin' to touch it, all that cryin' and wailing.

'I knew what it was then. I'd stepped into a place where something terrible had happened, or was goin' t' happen, either one, I don't know which, I couldn' tell which. An' it didn't matter. I was there, that's all.'

The silence that had fallen was intense. Langhurst, after a moment, looked away from Garrety, and Adair felt the youth's troubled gaze upon him, as if, with the advantage of age and authority, or some experience of a wider world, he might have something to say about this; then he turned back to Garrety, who, drawn and pale-looking, with the sweat standing out on his brow and his gaze turned inward, was still isolated in the midst of his vision, a horrified and unwilling witness.

'Well,' Langhurst said at last. 'That beats anything I ever heard. What did it mean?'

Garrety, stirring, shook his head, and swirling the last leaves in his pannikin, tossed them to the dark. It was a gesture that was meant to finish things. He had no more to tell.

Langhurst sat a little longer, fidgety, unsatisfied, reluctant to let Garrety slip back into his more familiar, uncommunicative self. He opened his mouth and seemed about to speak when another sound intervened.

Away to their left, outside their circle, a high-pitched wailing began, a weird sound, scarcely human.

Clearly it was the black, Jonas, who was making it; the top part of his body, where he sat cross-legged in the dust, was swaying. But the sound itself was coming from a point several feet beyond him, out of the earth, and as his voice shifted pitch, the sound too shifted, came from another

114

place altogether. Adair felt the hair rise at the back of his neck.

'Now look what you done,' Kersey whispered.

'It's all right,' Langhurst said, 'he's all right. I'll tend to him.'

Rising quickly, he went to where Jonas sat just beyond the light of the fire, and with a cracking of his knee-joints that was like gunshot in the hush that had fallen, or perhaps it was simply the intensity with which their ears were attuned, lowered himself and sat face to face opposite. There was just inches between them.

The wailing had increased and was leaping about from place to place, behind and in front of them, all at different pitches, peopling the night. In the midst of it the two figures, black and white, made a kind of balance.

It was Adair who thought this. What he could see from where he sat was the blond back of Langhurst's head, the thick hair rough-cut and greasy, and beyond, the wide-eyed, open-mouthed face of the black.

As if, he thought, the white youth were staring into a glass, and what looked back at him, though he appeared too calm to be surprised at it, was this black one distorted by horror or irreparable grief.

Then, as abruptly as it had begun, the wailing ceased, and for a time the two simply sat.

At last, a little awkwardly, Langhurst twisted his body, unflexed his knees, and got up.

Jonas continued to sit, staring trancelike ahead.

What a place this is, Adair thought, his eye on Jonas. God knows what things have happened here and gone unrecorded by men, or are on the way towards us. Will we ever know the true history of it? The secret history, stored away in the dark folds of the landscape, in its scattered bones, of a paradise found or lost. It struck him now that

115

the real difference between himself and these others was that he could leave the place, and would leave it, but that they belonged and would stick. What he could afford to raise as an interesting question was the ground of their lives.

'He's all right,' Langhurst was saying, his body suspended from a subdued, almost apologetic grin. 'He'll be quiet now.' He lowered himself and sat.

'That was a good trick,' Kersey said after a time. It was an unnecessary remark, and the moment it was out he knew it and looked embarrassed, but had needed, Adair saw, the reassurance of speech.

Langhurst did not respond. He looked very pale and unprotected. Very pure – that was the word that came to Adair's mind. Perhaps he had not known what he was going to do till he did it, but the impulse he had acted on was perfect, and the rightness of it assured him of something. He shone. So pleased with himself that he could not hide it. In a shy, surprised way, he grinned, then dropped his eyes and rubbed with the heel of his hand at a soft place on his thigh.

'Well,' Adair said, hauling himself upright. 'I'll be getting back.' Very briskly he began to issue instructions for the morning. A good length of rope, the digging of the grave. 'Be ready at half-past six,' he told them. 'I'll leave it to you, Kersey, to see that everything is prepared.'

'Right you are, sir, yessir, I'll see to it. You can depend on me.'

'Right then.'

He was about to turn away when Langhurst spoke.

'How is he then?' he asked.

His tone was neutral enough, but the boy, still in a heightened state after his performance was so open, so undefended, that you could see right into him, his broad face

116

flattened, washed with light. There was the tightness of real pain around his eyes.

He understood then that it was this one, not the other as he had thought, who was responsible for the beating Carney had taken. He felt sorry for the boy but what was there to say?

'He's been singing,' he told them.

Langhurst glanced at the others.

'Yes,' he said, 'we heard.'

With the open, hurt look still blunting his features he stood waiting, as if some explanation might be about to come forth, and Adair saw how strange it must have appeared, that sweet, unexpected singing.

'We thought,' the boy said, 'he might have been – you know, getting drunk.'

'No,' Adair said, 'but you remind me of something. Kersey, there's a bottle of rum in my knapsack. You'd better come and collect it. There'll be a good measure of it for you fellows in the morning' – he saw the quick looks that passed between them; so they were to be considered – 'a double shot for the prisoner.'

With this he felt free to move away.

'At half-past six, then,' Kersey was singing, delighted to have been singled out. 'On the dot! Don't you worry about a thing, sir. And I'll come for the other right away.'

7

HE MUST HAVE slept. His neck, when he shifted, was stiff where his head had rolled against the wall, one leg was cramped. He had no recollection of his dream. It was gone. Only the receding shadow of it still hung on and troubled him with the sense of something unfinished or not begun. He eased his leg, began to rub at the tight muscle. The light had burned out, but his eyes had now grown used to the dark. Carney too stirred. He began to mutter, then shouted a garbled phrase or two, and his eyes snapped open. He looked about wildly. They stared at one another.

The man did not know where he was. With the touch of fear still upon him, he was lost and sweating in whatever dark predicament he had been in just seconds ago and five feet from where Adair lay slumped in his own fitful sleep.

Adair's pulse began to race. Amazing that by some process of sympathetic understanding he could feel on the creeping surface of his skin the effect of the man's dream while having no conscious knowledge of it. And by what means could he have? How could he know what shadows, what old furies or figures of dread, as mysterious and personal as his own, haunted the man, and had followed him here? Yet here he was sweating in some new opening of understanding between them.

They continued to stare at one another, Carney's eyes troubled, directed inward. Whatever it was that lay upon him he had difficulty shaking it off. Could it be, Adair thought, the physical certainty at last of what was to occur? Which had come to him out of that deep body-knowledge that in sleep we have no guard against?

He shivered, and wondered if that, in one of its many hidden forms, had not been the substance of his own dream, which he recognized only now in the chill he felt, the goose-pimpling of his flesh.

'Cold, eh?' Carney said, hugging himself, his shoulders tense. 'It gets cold here in the early hours. It's a shock. The days are that blazing hot you don't expect it.'

Adair nodded. He could barely keep his teeth from chattering.

'I've never got used to it, I never adjusted. It's a different sort of cold – you know, to what I was used to. Up in the hills there, where we was hiding out, the nights got that cold it'd freeze the balls off you, it was like another hell. It's not the cold we was born to, you see. Back home – you know, in Ireland – I could go barefoot, sleep rough, it never bothered me.'

It's not the place, Adair thought. It's not the climate.

The man must have caught hold of the thought. He lowered his head and sat a moment with the great bulk of his skull sunk between his knees. The breath through his nose was raspy. 'It feels late,' he said at last. 'Do you by any chance have the time on you?'

Adair, sprawling at an awkward angle on the dirt floor, reached into a trouser pocket and drew out his watch.

It was a cheap one made of heavy alloy. There was a painted figure on the dial of a huntsman with a gun over his shoulder and at his heel a dog. It kept excellent time, but out of habit he held it to his ear before turning it to the weak light that flowed in from a crack in the door.

Twenty-eight minutes past three.

It seemed absurd in this place at the end of nowhere to

119

be so particular about the minute, to set a value on precision when nothing demanded that a man be punctual except habit, or the belief that his own dignity, proof of the stage he had reached in the order of God's creation, his grasp of the world's inevitable progress, was dependent on timing his every activity, on fitting every station of his daily progress, through mealtimes and labour and prayer and sleep, to the regularity with which the sun rolled round the heavens and the hands of a clock could divide up the vast distances it travelled into spaces of human dimension, minutes, seconds, in which a man could hold his breath. Time can be freedom, it can free us. Joy. How far he had got from the orderly universe at the Park.

Time was an obsession out here. He had thought it at first an anxiety, natural enough, about falling into the easy, un-British attitude of those who had wandered too far from Greenwich, or the many indolent and unreliable natives from India to the Caribbean and Brazil, who have never discovered its relation to lovely efficiency. But it had to do, he now believed, with something quite different – a preoccupation with space.

There was the usual strictness here in the matter of milestones and fences, which was only to be expected in a place that set itself to bring what was wild within the bounds of order and measurement. But when it came to acres, especially of pastoral land in places as yet unentered, numbers grew hazy. Five hundred could easily, when everything was as yet merely notional, become five thousand. And beyond that were spaces so vast that to measure them by striding out and numbering the strides made the mind quail – and how in that case could the body hold out? To keep track of the minutes in such a place was to stake out an area that could be contained, comprehended. So many hours, days, years to be got through till a sentence was served or grain could be cut and the land ploughed again for planting, or to set one row of bricks upon another and raise a courthouse, a prison, a decent habitation.

He was wandering. Looking up, he caught the keenness now with which Carney had his eye upon him.

– In his case, so many hours before the drop. Unforgivable that he should have kept the man hanging.

'Half-past three,' he said.

'Ah! I thought it would of been later.'

Poor fellow, he had longer than he thought. And in fact half past was itself an approximation. It was twenty-nine minutes past. He had a whole minute, sixty seconds more than he had been told. Should I inform him? Adair wondered. Will it make a difference? The last minute might – one more breath! But this one?

Of course neither this minute nor any of the minutes we have to get through between now and dawn mean anything special to me, Adair thought. And for one reason only. Because I have nothing to measure them against. Because, unlike this fellow here, I do not know, cannot guess, how much time has been allotted before the hour of my death.

Carney meanwhile, who appeared to have lost track of his sociable self, was shuffling about to get comfortable on the dirt floor, scratching, mumbling. His way, perhaps, like an animal, of settling, rasping a nail against some bit of the surface of his skin to remind himself of the familiarity of his body, finding, in the pleasurable response of the blood to this minor irritation, the reassurance that it was there.

Half-past three. Should I tell him? That the minute has ticked by? He was still holding the watch, feeling the metal beginning to warm in his hand. He leaned sideways – there was a pleasing pressure on the muscles of his hip, his body too was there – and put the watch away, but was still aware for a moment of its sturdy ticking.

121

It had been Paddy's; he had known it all his life. It was one of the first objects he had learned to love in his early days at Ellersley, and as a little lad of three or four had been allowed to sit up at the table in the big, stone-flagged kitchen and with the watch before him, without touching of course, follow the movement of the big hand round the dial. Follow too, as its shadow swept over them, the adventures, as he dreamed them up, of the huntsman and his dog, who were as real and familiar to him as the red-faced gamekeeper up at the Park, whose name was McManus and who had a dog called Flitch. But the hunts-man on the watch was not squat and round-headed like McManus, and did not wear leggings, but was a tall slim fellow in a blue jacket, with boots and a cocked hat with a feather, and had a sports-gun over his shoulder, a gamebag, and at his waist a flask, and the dog was a pretty Irish setter with one foot raised as it trotted beside him.

In the background was a tree with just a few leaves on it, which, when he learned to count, he had fixed at twenty – never more, never less; they did not fall. And there was a bird in the branches, but the huntsman did not see it, or if he did, was happy to let it be. It had its beak open, singing, and did not fly off.

All this close observation and careful accounting, mixed in as it was with dreamy reflection, had been the activity, he saw now, of a particular turn of mind, a particular way of dealing with the world: stolid, obsessive, but some other quality was there as well, though it was less easy to name and the contradiction it made was all his own.

Taking the watch out these days – it had been with him through all the years of his service, in Poland, in France, in the months he had spent in isolation as 'contagious officer' at the crossing on the Sava – was a reminder, if he needed one, of what was fixed and unchanging in him; the counterweight, there in his pocket, of his solemn self, a worn roundness he could reach for and weigh, heavy, crude, reliable, in his palm. It was some affinity he had recognized between them, rather than Adair's being so childishly fond of the thing, that had made Paddy leave it to him. Or so he sometimes thought.

It had sat on the table beside the old man's bed the night he was dying, fat, round, too loudly ticking in the high attic room. Beside it on the wooden table-top, a candle-snuffer in its tray, a glass of water with the smudge of the old man's saliva at the rim. He had gone up for just a moment to see how he was doing. 'I've been here since five,' the girl complained who had been set to sit with him. 'Is no one coming to relieve me?' He let her go, took her place on the chair, and the watch ticked out the minutes of his impatience to be away.

In the close heat under the roof there was a sour smell of sweat and old dirt, and with it another that he had not encountered till now, and which, as the old man breathed it out, was the smell, he knew, of corruption, of a death that had already begun in the lungs and, as it came out of the mouth and nostrils, carried to him, sitting close by on the rush-bottomed chair, an apprehension too immediate, too hotly personal, that he was in the presence of death. He sweated at the closeness of it. As if, just by allowing himself to come so near, by leaning down to the head on the pillow – the rheumy eyes raised to his own, their blue ringed with dirty white, the mottled brow, the weight of the skull making a hollow in the greyish pillow – by concentrating the whole of himself on what Paddy was trying, without success, to tell him, he had caught it, the contagion.

It was a foolish notion, and came, he knew, from his panicky fear. At nineteen, and preparing to be a soldier, he had thought enough of these things, though they had not till now registered themselves in the beating of his heart, the breaking out on his skin of cold sweat, to know that we catch that particular contagion with our first breath.

He continued to sit, and what struck him after a time, as Paddy dozed and his lean cheek hollowed and puffed a little with his breath, was the change in his old friend's features.

Refined of their coarseness, of their broad, peasant look – 'a good, old-fashioned Irish face,' Eamon Fitzgibbon would have said, 'with all the best in it of our stout Irish peasantry' – the sharp cheekbones and jaw with their white stubble, the cropped head, the veins at the temple, even the nest of hair in the nostrils and creeping out of his ears, resembled those of a knightly Earl Marshal or early saint; as if none of the old fellow's notorious oddities, his quirks of speech, his savagery at the expense of rivals, were to survive this common purging; as if no uncharitable reflection on the general character of men, no bitterness at what life had taught him, or curse at the wild injustice of things, had ever passed his lips. But they had! And as he sat listening to the long-drawn, rackety breath, which was like the noise some wooden contraption might make that had got out of kilter, he was determined to hang on to his own memory of them, not to allow this difficult nature, this old fellow who had loved him – and whom in his own way, which had too often been boyishly selfish and unseeing, he had loved in return – to be ennobled out of existence, made bland and acceptable. He laid the tip of his fingers to the old man's wrist, which was dark and hard as a twig. The bleared eyes rolled towards him.

'It's me,' he said. 'Michael.'

He felt obscurely that in insisting on his own identity, and in Paddy's coming back far enough to recognize it, he could make the old man reassume his own.

The eyes flickered. He pressed his fingers more deeply into the gristle between the bones.

What he wanted to say was: Tell me something, Paddy, something scandalous. Give me a bit of the old intolerant scorn. Call up the rats and weasels and the pigs in mud. Be your old irascible, unforgiving self.

The lips moved. Or he thought they did.

I may be dyin', but let's have no bloody tight-arsed angels in the room, little lily-white altar boys with the weasel in their britches, chantin' bloody responses at one end while the weasel goes its own way at the other.

He thought he heard Paddy's laugh.

He leaned forward to look at the watch. He had come in for just a moment. Half an hour had passed. He was expected at the Park at half-past nine. He, Fergus and Virgilia were to take advantage of the long midsummer evening with a picnic in the woods, with maybe a bathe afterwards in the stream. It was warm enough. He was aware of the air at the half-open window and the gathering sound, far off, of birds.

He was in his last week here and was determined, before he left, to speak openly to Virgilia and get something decided: their life, his fate, hers also. He had gone over and over what he would say to her. In some easy moment, under the influence of the summer night and his need at last to push things to the point; a moment when Fergus had wandered off, as he usually did, to pursue some interest of his own. If she was not too distracted by his absence, and, with their hair still wet from their bathe and the moon risen, the mood was right between them. Had prepared his mild answer to every question she might raise.

Each time he went over the encounter in his head it took a different direction, had a different shape, but he drove it, always, to the same conclusion.

He was filled with the optimism that came to him on the warmth of the summer night, from the clear light out there of the sky, and a light that was in him too, the physical assurance of youthful energy and of the way his life lay open before him even in the immediacy here of Paddy's reaching like a climber for every breath, and his own panicky sense of what it finally meant, and would mean to him too at last, to surrender to disintegration. But not yet! Not for years yet!

Quarter past. He would just have time to get there, but would have to run most of the way now, and would arrive red-faced and sweating. Never mind. He would be cool enough when it came to the time. Maybe the running would do him good. Take off some of his excitement. Already he leaned towards the exhilaration of it, felt its glow on his skin.

Paddy's eyes had been following his every movement. Now a look of terror came into them.

'What is it, Paddy?'

The old man, fearfully agitated, began to shake his head and tried to raise a hand. When Adair took it, it closed on his own with a grip as of death itself. He was astounded at the dying man's strength.

'What is it?' he asked again.

But he knew the answer already.

'It's all right,' he said, 'I won't leave you.' Is that it? Is that it, Paddy?

The grip loosened, and he sat while the watch ticked away, louder than ever it seemed: past the quarter, on to the half. The hand, relaxed now, in his own. Past ten. On to eleven.

They would not have waited more than an hour. They would be out in the woods, the cloth gleaming white in the still transparent dark, the moist air drenched with the smells

126

of summer, wormwood, elder-flower, the overpowering, far-travelling sweetness of lime-blossom. They would bathe in the stream, calling to one another in the dark as they shared its coolness. They would dress again in the cover of a hedge, and emerge refreshed and with their hair dripping. He had a vision of Virgilia leaning over to wring the water from her hair, then laughing and throwing back her head. They would walk back slowly, hand in hand, to where the cloth gleamed like another pool they might plunge into.

In the heady warmth, with moonlight playing in the leaves overhead and the scent of lime-flower to lead them, mightn't their hands find one another – innocently at first, then with a quickening awareness as their palms grew moist, their blood beat faster? Fergus would know well enough where this was leading. He was not innocent. He had been more than once to the maids' room down the corridor under the roof. That was natural enough, he was fifteen. And she? Hadn't he seen the face of desire in her? He watched Fergus take her hand and place it on his breast, then raise it and set her soft palm to his lips. Then tilt his head forward, set his mouth against her neck. – I must go, he thought, I must, I must!

He jerked away, but the dry hand tightened on his own, and it was too late, he saw. If all this had unfolded as his heated brain had imagined it, then it was already too late, and had always been. He groaned and sank into an agony of his own, but did not attempt to break Paddy's grip.

After a little, Clarke, one of the footmen, came with a candle, and he sent him to call Mama Aimée. 'Has he had the last rites?' he asked when she arrived.

'Father Egan was here at eight,' she told him. 'I'm surprised you didn't pass him on the stairs. I told them to call me if he was any worse.' She sat on the far side of the bed and took Paddy's hand. 'Yes,' she said when he turned towards her. 'It's me, my old darling. *And* Michael. We won't leave you.'

He died, after a fearful struggle, about four in the morning. There was nothing noble in it. A demented animal hurling itself again and again against the bars of a cage. Mama Aimée had wept on his shoulder – Paddy had been part of her childhood as he had been part of his own. He too wept. For Paddy. Out of nervous exhaustion. For his lost chance . . .

'Excuse me, sir.'

It was Carney.

'Are you in pain?'

'Me? No. Why do you ask?'

'You were sort of groanin'. I thought, sir, you might be in pain.'

'No. I must have dozed off.'

'I was goin' to ask you something, I hope you don't mind.' He rubbed his nose very vigorously with the back of his fist. 'Do you think, sir,' he said after a moment, 'that there is such a thing as forgiveness?'

Adair stared at the man, unable for a moment to focus his mind.

'I mean – you know, for what we done.'

He found his voice after a moment but it was thick with emotion. 'I'm sure there is,' he said. He was thinking still of Paddy. 'If there isn't, there is no hope. None. For any of us.'

The man nodded, but in his scrupulous way was not convinced.

'I don't just mean, you know, our bits of pleasure and that – they can't grudge us those, do you think, sir?'

Pleasure! The word was so unexpected it sent a rush of heat to his heart and he felt a fierce throb of desire that came from nowhere; but wasn't it always like that? – the urge, the yearning, so sudden and inappropriate, cutting in across a man's every attempt to be rational or serious; out of some vision caught in a fugitive way in the street, and which only the blood recalls, of a bit of women's clothing hung out on a line and seductively shifting; an episode from the body's anarchic other-life, desires, lusts that a man has incessantly to beat down in a world where there is no place for such wayward stirrings, or only such crude ones as fill him afterwards with the shame of unrestraint and loss.

'Oh,' the man said, concerned that Adair might have taken him amiss, 'I didn't just mean – you know, women. Other pleasures. Like just bein' idle like, with nothin' to do but get drunk in the sun. But women too, I can't deny that. Even if it is a sin as they say, it's a man's nature. An' God knows, it wasn't that many, and I can't say even now that I'm sorry for it.'

'Why should you?' Adair said, almost brutally. 'Why should you?'

'If it's a sin, sir, as they say.'

Adair made a dismissive motion with his hand. It might have meant anything but Carney now was alert.

'You don't believe in it? In sin?'

'I don't know,' Adair said. 'I can't answer all these questions you keep putting to me. How could I? I'm not a priest.'

Carney drew back, and he was immediately sorry for his outburst. 'No,' he said very firmly, 'to be truthful I do not. I do not believe in it. Not at all.'

Carney looked surprised at his vehemence, and the fact was, he was surprised himself. Something in the turn the conversation had taken disturbed him. He felt a kind of anger at the world of denial he had glimpsed in the misery of the man's poor confession. Such common delights – why the denial? Why should ordinary fellows crawling about under the sun begrudge themselves these innocent comforts in a world that was so full of injustice and every sort of misery? Why was he – for it was himself he was thinking of – so ashamed of these disorderly surges of a desire that was, after all, what kept the world itself in existence, or all the part of it, at least, that was human; kept humanity, in all its irrepressible millions, breathing and pushing for place, for a little light and air, a little dignity too, before it was crushed back into the dust; kept it hanging on, like this fellow here, to a few more hours of warmth in the flesh. A mere momentary excitation of the nerves, a brilliant bewilderment that could mean much or little – wasn't that a small consolation for so much striving to keep the body clothed and fed, for so much close-mouthed endurance and back-breaking toil and stumbling blindly from one moment to the next?

'A hundred years from now men will live very different lives from anything we know, Michael.' That is what Eamon Fitzgibbon had told him. 'The world will be transformed. *We* will be transformed. The process has already begun – I saw it myself, the beginning – August the fourth, 1789. Your children and grandchildren, in 1910, 1915, will be in the glorious midst of it. Our lives, child, yours and mine, are what must go into the making of it, as the lives of all the generations before us, sunk deep in mud and filth but painfully climbing out of it, have made all this, all these books on the shelves here, and what is in them, a good fireplace and a fire that draws, those andirons, these solid walls that keep the weather out and make a place for pictures to hang, that fine shirt you are wearing, those stout boots, the oil that goes into this lamp so that we can read our Plutarch and all that the men of these latter days have given us, the order and beauty of their minds, as an example of the order we must create in our own, then in the world around us . . .'

He was just fourteen. He sat listening in the dim light of the Library, seated in a body that was all turmoil, all disorder, blind lust, so that for all the time Eamon Fitzgibbon was urging him to a vision of truth and justice in a time to come, his own backward nature, which knew and cared nothing for reason, drew him back to the dirty footsoles of the servant girl he had seen on the stairs on the way up as she knelt at her scrubbing: the light of her thighs, where she had hoicked up her skirt and it rode higher each time she lunged forward and swung her arm in a half-circle leaving a swathe of suds; her raised rump, and when he turned back, the way her eyes had lifted to his, moist with the headcold that made her sniff and draw the back of her hand across her nose.

She was his own age. He had seen her before but did not know her name. That she had seen so clearly what was in his mind made her even more desirable to him. Her dirty feet. The moist sound of the mucus in her nose. His cock had puffed and thickened, grown so tight with blood that as he went on up he had had, furtively, to push it into a less visible position in his breeches.

The image had stayed with him, and not only through the following lesson. It had continued to feed his senses in solitary moments when he had only to reach for it and the pleasure he rose to was once again that of the fourteen-year-old who had been stopped dead, his body aflame, by the choking closeness of it. And who knows? Perhaps it was because the image was forever associated with them, that for all his distraction, Eamon Fitzgibbon's words had struck so deeply into his soul.

'We have come only a little way, child, there is still all about us so much ignorance – look at us here in Ireland! –

so much misery and hunger. In your lifetime, Michael, all this will change, and more swiftly than any man could have believed when I was your age. Ignorance will vanish, disease, crime, hunger. Men will no longer be at one another's throats. I believe all this. I know it is true. I envy you the world you will see. God may exist – I do not deny that, though as you know I am no great friend of the Church – and be responsible for all this. But in that case he is responsible for the evil as well as the good and has great need of us. It is our business to make good his mistakes, to achieve, as far as we are able, that just world of perfect reason and order that He, for whatever reason, has failed to provide for us. Perhaps because the greater glory is to stand by and let His creatures do it through the gifts He has given us.'

He had struggled. He had sat for long hours beside the candle with the pages burning before him, trying to get into his head and make live there a belief in the forces of order and justice that would transform their lives, and had felt, with a deepening sadness, that the venture must be fruitless, because it had already and so clearly failed in him: and where else could it begin but with particular cases, in individual bodies and souls?

He remained lumpishly untransformed. More insistent than his love of justice, or his will to achieve it, was the need to relieve himself savagely of the vision of that girl's thighs, whose light was so much more dazzling than the light off any page, and the darkness between them so close to a form of darkness in himself that he clung to and would not relinquish. For there were moments when he loved his body. For all its betrayals, for all its secret dedication to disorder, he truly loved it. It was his way into the world. All his affection for things, all that was most tender in him, came through it. Not through what he knew, or even what he believed and had failed to grasp or love enough, but, bewildering as it was, through what this lump of flesh told him.

'Are there no crimes, then?'

'What?'

'Crimes. Half of us in this country are here for the crimes we done.'

'There are crimes, yes. Of course there are. There's the law. Men make that and then punish those who break it.'

Adair, in the cool precision of this, felt the wave of sensuality that swept over him, and which must, he thought, have been the last flushings of his unremembered dream, recede, drain away, leaving him calm but exhausted.

'I don't know,' Carney muttered. 'Half the time, when I broke it, I didn' even know what it was. How could I? They never even learned me what it was. I had to live. I *had* to break it. I wonder I didn' do worse than I did, considerin'. I was an animal half the time, no better, no worse. But how could I of been otherwise? There's such a thing in the world as hunger. But was we any better when we was brought here, an' hung up in the triangles and whipped? Not a bit of it. Worse if anything, worse I'd say. The fact is, sir' – he was becoming more and more agitated – 'I killed a feller, I killed a man. That's what I wanted to tell you.'

With the light full in his face so that all his bruises showed, one eye half-closed in the puffy, iridescent flesh, he wore a pitiful expression. They had arrived all in a rush at something ultimate. The mere statement seemed to have drawn all the air out of the man's lungs. He seemed on the point of choking. He had let something loose between them, some phantom or fury, that terrified him.

'When you were out there?' Adair found himself asking. A jerk of his head indicated the invisible ranges.

'No, not then. I never killed no one then. They say I did

133

but it's a lie, there's a lot that's not true in what they say. I did not.'

'But some of the others did. Dolan did.'

The question side-tracked him completely. He looked puzzled. 'Ah,' he moaned at last, 'what's the point of goin' over all that? He paid for it, if 'e did, poor darlin'.'.

The anguish of this, the old Irish endearment, shamed Adair. He dropped his gaze, but for a moment had felt his heart leap. In that moment he had got very close. Some shadow of Fergus had passed between them.

'I won't say no more o' that,' Carney muttered.

He let his head fall between his knees and a great sob came out of him that made the powerful shoulders heave. He dashed the back of his hand across his eyes. 'No,' he said, recovering his voice, 'this was before all that.

'Do you know a place called Camden, sir? I was sent there with a road-gang. We was puttin' a road through. There was this feller, Shafto they called 'im. From Newcastle, what they call a Geordie. Skinny little runt, as black as any man I ever see. They say 'e was a miner. He looked like the coal-dust had got right into 'im, he was that black. Well, he took a dislike to me. It'll happen sometimes, a feller'll take a dislike. No reason. Or not one you'd ever get to the bottom of. It wasn't for any harm I ever done 'im. I'd barely looked at him. Barely knew 'e was there. But it made 'im mad, like, just bein' in the sight of me. I knew it an' kept out of 'is way. You get to reckernize such things in a man, livin' the life I did. If you don't you're in trouble. Anyway, I seen it an' kept out of 'is way. On'y I couldn't always. We was in the same gang. An' the fact is, it didn' suit 'im. 'E'd seek me out. The sight of me maddened 'im but that was just what he wanted. 'E couldn' let me be.

'I'd be sittin' over me bit o' food, where we were all eatin' together in a ditch, an' I'd look up an' there 'e'd be.

He'd of moved just so's 'e could get a better look at me. He'd be starin' like, with the food in his mouth half-eaten. It meant more to 'im, that – what 'e had against me – than gettin' the food into his mouth. Well, I knew sooner or later 'e'd have a go at me. Bound to, I thought. Well, that's all right, I thought, you do it, I'll be ready for ye. There was no point, you see, in arguin'. I knew that. It was just the way 'e was. The way I was too, what could I do about it? I wasn't livin' my life to please him.

'Well, there was another feller in the gang. A kid, really. Girlish sort o' lad, a bit light in the head if you know what I mean, but no harm in 'im. This other feller, this Shafto, took to tauntin' 'im. Not bullying like – more taunting, which can be worse sometimes. It made the rest of us uncomfortable. What 'e was suggestin', like. These things do go on, you know, sir – men are animals, there are fellers that do such things, it's best not to speak of 'em. I never had nothin' to do with that sort o' thing meself, nor the lad neither – or if 'e did, I never knew it. It was just that 'e was delicate like, soft. It made some men kinder to 'im, others the opposite. It's strange that, how one man'll go one way, another just the opposite. Anyway, it upset me, his tauntin' the lad like that, an' when he saw it he was pleased. Sort of – satisfied. I saw the little smile on 'is face. He'd found a way of gettin' at me. So I thought, it'll do me no good to say anything, it'll on'y make matters worse. So from then on there was two of 'em I had to keep out of the way of.'

He paused, wet his lower lip, frowning. Chewed a moment at the hangnail of his thumb.

'You know, sir, there's some things seem like fate. Whatever step you take, in any direction, there it is right in front of you, it can't be avoided. He didn' give up, that feller. He

135

just went on and on, and one day I just said, "Leave it alone," I said, "why don't you?" Not loud.

' "What was that?" he says back, gleeful like but tryin' to keep it hid. He was that happy. It had come at last.

' "We all know," he says, in a voice he was tryin' like to keep steady, he was that worked up, "we all know why you're speakin' up for the cunt." Then he said somethin' I wouldn't want to repeat.

'I didn't think. I just threw meself right at 'im. He was smaller than me. He must of known if we fought I could beat the daylight out of 'im. I meant to kill him, I can admit that. I wanted to stamp 'im right into the ground. Like you would a spider. I hit him, he went down. I didn't need to 'ave hit 'im again. I've got a temper, like. It comes on quick but it goes off quick as well, an' it 'ad gone off, so I didn't need to 'ave hit him again. But I did, an' I put the whole weight of me body into it. I wanted to knock 'im out of the light.' He sat shaking his head. 'I said I meant to kill 'im and I did mean it, then I didn't. An' it was when I didn't, an' didn' need to, that I went in an' finished 'im off. Deliberate. Some part of me just hit out and did it, an' I stood back with the sweat flyin' off me, and to tell God's truth, sir, I never felt better in all me life.'

He paused, sat back a little. There was an air of cold defiance in him.

'So,' he said. 'What do ye make a' that?'

'What did the magistrate make of it?'

Carney gave a rough laugh. 'Never made nothin' of it, didn' get the chance to. That night I used a file an' got away. Spent four days in the bush round there – they hunted me all over, dogs an' all – then got away and over the range.'

'And met up with Dolan.'

'That's right. After a bit I did, but I was on me own at

136

first. Three weeks it was. I was half starved and more or less out o' me wits when they come acrost me.'

'And what did Dolan make of it?'

'What do you mean?'

'Your story. Didn't you tell it to him?'

The look Carney gave him suggested there was something he had not understood.

'No sir, I never told no one till now.'

'Because you were ashamed?'

'No, sir,' he said very simply, but with a weary impatience as if, once again, Adair had failed to understand. 'Because I *wasn't*.'

There was a long pause.

'So then,' he repeated. 'What do you make of it?'

He wants me to tell him he was right, Adair thought. No, not that. He wants absolution.

'I told you before,' he said. 'I'm not a priest.'

'I know that, sir. I'm askin' you as man to man. You've been very patient with me, sir, listenin' an' that. I've never had much of a chance till now – you know, to talk things over. I'd like to know your opinion.'

'Of what you did?'

'Yes, sir. Of me, sir.'

Adair drew a deep breath. When he spoke it was for himself as much as for the other.

'If I were God,' he began – It is an illusion, he thought, this faith we have in reason, this conviction that we can keep disorder at bay by making rules and twisting our nature out of the way it would lead us; into the most horrible crimes perhaps, but they would be *our* crimes, the ones our nature demands. Instead of which, we live in the shadow of the crime not committed, though we still bear the guilt of it. In obedience to the rules. And our cowardice festers in us, turns our whole nature awry in a parody of what it means to be guiltless. There is no answer to this, but everything we think of as human and civilized depends upon it. 'If I were God,' he said again, 'I would choose to forgive because I could not find it in my heart to do otherwise.'

Carney looked up at him. His expression was one of pathetic gratitude.

'Thank you, sir.'

'For what? I am not God.'

'I know that, sir.' He considered a moment. 'Do you think, sir, that that is how it will be? You know, afterwards.'

Adair shook his head. 'I can't answer that, Carney. You ask me questions I can't answer. You wanted me to answer as a man. Well, that's it, that's my answer.'

Time enough, he thought, for the other, later on.

Which is what Daniel Carney too might have been thinking.

8

ONE OF THE things that most perplexed him, and the more as he grew older and saw the signs of it in so many places, felt in himself the ever-present slide towards it, was what it might be in the world that made disintegration an essential element of existence – that slow process of breaking up, falling apart, which, once it has begun, and once you have become aware of it, seems ever quickening and inevitable, and which, only when you have ceased to fear the personal effect of it, that is, when you can observe it from a distance in others, can be looked upon as touching, and regretfully, stoically, accepted.

When, he wondered, looking back, did he first feel the presence of it as a force in the lives they lived at Ellersley? When he was twelve? When he was fifteen? The insecurity of his place there had always, it seemed to him, made its customs and habits, its seasonal routines and fixtures, almost painfully precious to him. He clung to them with a childish anxiety, determined to keep up each one of them, even when others, like Mama Aimée, seemed happy to let them go. It was an aspect perhaps of what they called old-fashioned in him, this nostalgia for abidingness, this solemn preoccupation, even when he was himself a green little thing, growing and hungering for life, with the preservation of all that was settled, with what you could hope to find tomorrow where you had left it yesterday.

In fact no place he could have chosen was better designed

than Ellersley to frustrate and deny him. Each year the old order there, such as it was, or such as he had imagined it to be, was more deeply shaken. Some of this, he knew, was general, the slow accumulation of grime and verdigris and rust, the building up of more rubbish, more of the detritus of living, than could be packed into boxes and pushed out of sight, or hauled across the yard and sent up in a column of smuts. But the rest was personal. It had to do with the nervous insecurities of Mama Aimée, which each year made her more wild and unpredictable, and the indolence and empty self-importance of the man who called himself the master and who occasionally, and disastrously, appeared in that role, but whose only contribution to the household was the mess he made and his complaints afterwards, which were loud and circumlocutory, against Mama Aimée's timidity in dealing with Paddy and that ignorant fellow's connivance with the servants in every sort of slatternliness and Irish indiscipline.

He appeared at Ellersley less often now, and when he did there was no longer between him and Mama Aimée the old easy accord that had made them, despite all, a couple who, so long as they were in the same room together, could barely keep their hands off one another – to the point sometimes of public amusement and scandal. She had lost patience at last: with his infidelities, his debts, the assumption in the man of fifty that he was the same engaging fellow she had been so taken with at nineteen, and had only to show her the smallest sign of affectionate interest to win her indulgence for any folly, any betrayal.

Perhaps what she could not forgive in him was something she could see clearly now because it was reproduced, though in a different form, in Fergus, and was hard on Fergus because she recognized in him the charm of the father and would not be fooled a second time.

As for James Connellan, deeply hurt that his good nature, which was real, should be rejected after so long, he grew first resentful, then belligerent, but fell back at last on a natural indifference. He no longer tried to keep things up to the mark. So long as there was food on the table and whiskey to drink, he raised no questions and turned a blind eye to the many manifestations of a growing disorder; sat up at night with his cronies playing cards or leading them, armed with candelabra, in madcap races across the lawn, slept till noon, strode about in a quilted gown giving unnecessary orders to impress his friends with his authority as master, then rode off again.

Mama Aimée had simply withdrawn even further into herself. She was more often than ever in a 'condition'. Paddy continued to bully her, but he himself was older, more forgetful, less able to rule.

Terrible wars raged in the kitchen. Mrs Upshaw, after days of spying and counting and re-counting the napkins or measuring the tea in her caddies, would launch into hysterical accusations against one or other of the servants. An inquisition would be held that involved tears and bad language of a kind that would never previously have been tolerated, and one or more of the servants, a stuttering footman it might be, or a voluble but dim scullery maid, would be disgraced and, since Mama Aimée had no wish to see them punished, consigned to destitution.

'Don't tell me about these things,' Mama Aimée wailed, 'I don't want to know what's going on down there, Paddy. That's your affair.'

Whole families of beggars, foul-mouthed, brutal-looking people, barefoot and in rags, with neither work nor shelter, would refuse to be dealt with at the kitchen door where Paddy stood shouting and came swarming into the yard.

They snatched at Mama Aimée's leather stirrup, and holding up small children like sickly dolls with their heads lolling, raised their voices in a general wail. 'Paddy, this is shameful,' Mama Aimée would complain, genuinely distressed, for she was always full of compassion, but terrified as well by the clamour and by so many dirty, upraised hands. 'Why aren't these people being dealt with decently?' The dogs would be moiling about, yelping and showing their teeth.

The dogs too were out of control. At times, with Fergus driving them, they would come bounding up the steps and break in a pack into the hall, their claws sending them slipping and sliding, all floppy-eared, over the marble floor. Up the stairs they plunged, to run in and out of the rooms, sniffing at corners, peeing against the walls. There would be uproar as the younger footmen, who thought it a great lark, rushed here and there trying to catch and hold them, at last running them out again and to their kennels across the yard.

Eamon Fitzgibbon, hearing tales of a crisis, sent his steward De Vere across to make sense of the accounts, which Mama Aimée insisted on managing herself. They spent an hour locked up in her floral writing-room, and the De Vere who emerged was like a man who had seen the apocalypse.

'Poor Mr de Vere,' she told them at dinner. 'He was rather overcome by my *system*. He talked round and round in such a complicated way. In an absolute terror, I think, of being – comprehended. As if I'm such a fool that I don't know, haven't known for ages, that Mr Connellan has ruined us. Yes, that's the truth of the matter, but what's to be done about it? We must go on. You would have thought they were spiders instead of just a column of figures, the way the poor man jumped when he looked at them. I told him, I'm not afraid of crises, Mr de Vere, any more than I am of spiders. I'm not one of your crewel and cambric creatures. I've been dealing with crises for thirty years.'

Fergus meanwhile, at sixteen, was a man. Already over six feet three and no longer amenable to discipline, he was allowed to go about pretty much as he pleased, had his own horses, his own pack of harriers; barelegged, dishevelled, he came and went according to his own wishes and ignored even his mother's easy regimen.

Only on the rarest occasions now did Mama Aimée decide to make an effort and invite company. The call would go out to Mrs Upshaw to deploy her forces. Servants would be despatched to wash the walls down where the dogs had pissed. Buckets of suds would be sluiced over the marble floor of the entry-hall and three or four girls from the kitchen would slosh about on their knees with a scrubbing brush. Adair would be sent to find Fergus, with an order that he was to clean up and make himself presentable.

It was Adair's nature to hold himself apart, so far as he could, from the new disorder. He stepped over the messes the dogs had left, turned aside when he heard shouting on the stairs, since it was Mama Aimée and Fergus these days who were involved in the public altercations there that sent chambermaids scurrying for cover and made footmen pause and creep backwards through a door. Now that he had lost all power to deal between them he preferred not to listen.

He had only a limited influence over Fergus, and since the one appeal he could make involved old affections between them that he felt were sacred and should not be resorted to for the often trivial demands that Mama Aimée was likely to make, he avoided her commissions and no longer bullied Fergus on her behalf. But he could not always escape.

'You look like one of the stable-boys,' he told him as

143

dirty-faced, his stockings round his ankles, his hair loose where the knot that tied it had come undone, he rolled about with one of the dogs licking his face.

He sat up, or tried to, pushing the big dog off.

'Enough now, Cinna. Enough!' and he wrestled the dog and threw it aside. It landed on all fours and crouched expectantly. 'Enough,' he said, panting, and sat pushing his damp hair back into the knot.

'You'd better wash and get changed,' Adair said lightly. 'The McMahons are coming.'

'Damn the McMahons!' He rolled on his back, and laughing, let the big dog lap his cheek. 'Honestly, Mickey, be honest now, do you really care what Milly McMahon thinks? She's a stupid bitch, and so are Alice and Emma, and Charlie's worse. Stupid. The lot of them.'

'Mama Aimée will be upset, that's all.'

He turned away.

'What you really mean is, you want to make a good impression on Charlie McMahon. God only knows why. He's an idiot. All he ever thinks about, the great ox, is the buttons on his waistcoat and the set of brushes his godfather sent him.'

It was all very well for him, Adair thought. He never tried to make an impression, good or bad, cared for no one's opinion, but the McMahon girls just the same were besotted with him. They found his scowls Byronic, hung on his moody silences. When he broke into smiles, because his natural charm and good humour could not long contain itself, they thought him the most delightful boy in all Ireland. It wasn't true what people said of him. That he was half savage and unfit for society.

It made no difference that he had not washed or changed his shirt. Some grace had been afforded him that belonged so completely to his nature that he had never considered it, may even have thought it so general as to be beyond consideration. Adair, who had spent every day of his life with him, and would have known immediately if there was any element of calculation or self-consciousness in him, had no more resistance to it than the latest appearing and most unreflective stranger.

'Well,' he said now, 'have it your own way. I won't argue with you.'

'Oh, all right then. For you, Mickey, if it's going to fret you.' He pushed the dog off, got to his feet. 'Don't be angry with me. But honestly, the McMahons! Tell Mason to fetch me a clean shirt. I'll wash in the yard,' and with Cinna flopping at his heels he bounded off to douse his head and shoulders at the pump where Paddy washed the cart. He towelled himself down with the shirt he was wearing and came back shining.

And now it was Virgilia who pressed him at every moment to know where Fergus had got to, why she never saw him, what he thought, what he felt.

'Why do you ask me these things?' Adair said. 'You're closer to him than I am.'

He saw the little burst of pleasure this gave her.

'Am I?'

'You should ask *him* these things.'

'You know why I don't.'

He turned away. She knew him too well; he would not let her see his smile of satisfaction.

It was her transparency that made him cruel.

They saw more of each other than ever, he and Virgilia. He caught at every glimmer of feeling in her, read every novel she dropped a hint of, seeking greedily what her eye might have found there, training himself in the pursuit of feelings, and little twists and turns of feeling, to guess what it was in this or that episode she had mentioned that had struck her, searching out her sticky fingerprints and the catches of her breath so that he could know more intimately how her heart moved, and the secret signs by which she told what she did not intend to tell or what, when she told it, she meant no one to hear, and was disconcerted when, as often happened, she appeared to confound with her lightness his deep discoveries.

'Honestly, Michael, you weren't really impressed by that foolish Amalie.' They were talking of the heroine of a new novel. 'She's a goose. Perfect – pluperfect! I don't believe she's ever had the experience, poor girl, of an uncooked turnip or a dirty stocking. Are only those who are blessed with nerves, or fading away with interesting diseases, to come into the light? Are we doomed by fresh air and the amount of potatoes we put away, you too, Michael' – she clasped his hand and for a moment her body swung lightly towards him – 'to remain forever healthy and dull? Except, as you know, for the chickenpox we had together when we were seven I've been well for the whole of my life and mean to stay that way. Is good spirits and high ideals an impossible combination?'

Her tone of gentle mockery was intended, he saw, to be a rebuke to something in himself rather than a revelation of what he had failed to perceive in her. He knew the quality of her spirit already, her brightness and good health. What dismayed him was the implied criticism of his own.

She had sides – that's what she wanted him to see, but he knew it already; and some of them were turned away from him. Well, he had begun to see that too.

Though the housekeeper at the Park was perfectly competent, she liked, for example, to be on duty on big wash-days when, after a week of cloud-watching and divination and argument and postponement, the coppers were filled, starch made, and great snowy piles of linen appeared over nearly half an acre of lawn and bushes, growing lighter and more airy with every watchful minute till, the unpredictable sky taking a turn for the worse and the housekeeper having tested a pillowcase against her cheek, the signal went out and droves of chambermaids and kitchen girls and footmen were sent scurrying from bush to bush, like peasants getting the harvest in under a threat of hail, but in a holiday mood of light-hearted hilarity as they plucked up table-cloths, napkins and armfuls of bed-linen, darting easily out of one another's path in a kind of dance or deliberately, deliciously colliding.

She had a different look on these occasions from the Virgilia he knew from the Library or in the ballroom or on their outings to horse-trials or county fairs. She was at the centre of a world whose activities and forms – the bottling of fruit from the orchard, the making of crab-apple jelly and elderberry wine – demanded a competence, a judgement about the consistency of a syrup or the setting-point of a jam, that she appeared to have acquired from nowhere. Except that she hadn't of course. He saw from the way the underwomen looked to her for judgement that her experience was trusted and her competence old. It was the first indication he had had that the world she shared with Fergus and himself, and which he had taken as all-embracing, was not the only area in which her ready spirit worked – or her mind, either. It was, he thought, something picked up from her domestic concerns, another rhythm, another way of seeing, that was behind the things she said that most surprised him, even when the domestic as he understood it was at the furthest distance from what they had in hand.

'The tendency of all things, you know, isn't towards extinction – that is what you think, isn't it?'

147

'What?' he asked.

'I've noticed. You act always, I've seen it, as if the essential movement in things is a kind of running down. I suppose that comes from physics, but it comes from something else too – your mind being so fixed on the body. You take that as the model of *everything*.'

'Do I?' he said, genuinely surprised. He blushed. Had she seen that he was only half-listening? While she spoke of tendencies and physics, he had chiefly been aware of the pressure of her palm against his own – the warmth of it, this outpost of her body's heat.

'Well, don't you? And because you believe the only end of everything is extinction you can't wait to prove it so, and since it can't be avoided, you grow more and more impatient for it, you can't wait for it to be consummated. There's the whole principle of masculine activity!'

'Has this got something to do,' he asked, 'with my going away to be a soldier?'

'No,' she told him, 'it has not. You take everything back to yourself.' He accepted this; admiring, as always, the spiritedness of her attack. She was so utterly present, mind and body, in everything she did. 'It's got to do with the way the world is. The real movement, I think, is towards refinement, towards the essence, something so fine that we think it is gone but all it has done, in fact, is become more absolutely itself. There's no question of extinction!'

'And where did you hear all this?'

'I worked it out – oh, from quite practical cases, I assure you. I do *think*, you know.'

'Too much,' he found himself saying.

'No, not too much. I don't think about myself – except as an example like the rest. I think but I don't rationalize,' she explained. 'It isn't a straight line, it's all – leaps.'

'Do I think in a straight line? Is that what you're saying?'

'No,' she said. 'I would rather say, in a circle.'

'Is that good or bad?' He was quite at sea.

'Well, it's nicer than a straight line, my dear. Or anyway, I like it better. But I can't say your captain when you are in the army will prefer it.'

They spent long hours walking hand in hand in the Park or sitting at the end of the matchwood pier. Anyone observing them might have seen in it the intimacy of a loving pair who could not get enough of one another's company, and in a way, it was true, they were. But if her eyes lit up at his appearance in a doorway to interrupt her reading, or if, glancing up from her favourite spot on the ornamental bridge, she saw him emerging from the woods, it was, he knew, because she would be free now to speak of Fergus, to excite herself, before their time together was quite over, by having his name upon her lips. And if he tormented himself by indulging her, it was because, in allowing her this opportunity to pursue her passion, he could, in the sound of her voice, so vibrant and full of feeling, in the sight of her profile as she walked beside him, so easily gratify his own.

They had much to talk of. Fergus, who could never be relied upon to turn up when he promised or to stay when he did, had developed a life apart from theirs that was a constant puzzle to them. Not in its details, since he hid nothing from them of the names and occupations of his new companions, but in what it was that drew him. This he could not express, or would not.

'What do you mean?' he would ask. 'They're friends, that's all.' The attempt to get at his reasons, to make motives of what, from his point of view, was mere whim or interest, went against the grain with him as he grew more and more to distrust words, and more often than ever now escaped, even when he was with them, into that distance that had always enraged Virgilia, or later, when she had learned to disguise it, threw her into an unaccustomed panic, and which Adair had accepted ages ago as a line between them that could not be crossed.

His new companions were daredevils and rowdies, ungovernable youths not much older than himself, the sons of the Galway gentry, or young lawyers – clerks from town, who swore deep allegiance and played at conspiracy and led one another when they were drunk into the sort of talk that a generation before had bathed the whole country in blood.

Virgilia was fiercely admiring of such rebel passions, and if women had been included might have been one of them, a leader even and more ardent than the rest. But women were not included, and it vexed her that Fergus, out of loyalty to his friends, and a boyish delight in oaths and cabals, would do no more than hint at what was in the wind.

Wild-eyed, tongue-tied fellows would appear at Ellersley and stand, cap in hand, till he came out and spoke to them; fellows with straw in their hair, who travelled to county fairs and brought him news, or so they claimed, of horses he might be interested in, in villages forty miles off in another county. He would ride off with them and be gone whole nights and days, looking, when he got back, as if he had slept in ditches or been in a brawl. Mama Aimée raged. James Connellan, preoccupied as always with his own affairs, shrugged his shoulders; the boy was his own master. Virgilia, for whom he had become the agent of her own spirit of rebellion and heroic adventure, was torn between frustration that he was never there when she wanted him and an impatient wish to have him range out, return and lay his exploits at her feet. If she could not ride with him she could at least be the sharer of his secrets.

He did come to them with his tales. He was too open in his nature, they were too close, all three, for him to keep them entirely to himself. But she felt always that she had failed to get to the bottom of things; that even in the telling of them, even as he lay just as she had dreamed, with his head in her lap while she stroked his hair, there was something he held back, some intimate involvement of himself that he deliberately kept hidden, or which she could not grasp because he could not express it.

But nothing, Adair saw, was held back. Did she, for all her longing to dive into his soul, know so little of him? His withdrawals to the margin of himself were a form of unreflective dreaming, not the expression of a nature that was close or politic. He threw himself into things, boldly, impetuously, and did not ask what it was in himself that his recklessness reflected, what shadows, larger than action itself, might be at work to drive him on. And it was these and these only that Virgilia wanted to share with him. But how can he reveal them to her? Adair thought. He does not even know they are there.

When he was gone there was, once again, just the two of them, to go over and over what he had told, drawn closer by his absence.

They knew him better, each in their different way, than he knew himself. They were, as he showed them often enough, two of a kind, as like one another as he was different.

'I should break with all this,' Adair told himself, 'and I will, I will! But not yet.'

There was a quality of abjection in it that he knew was unmanly and of which he ought to be ashamed. But the sweetness of his suffering was a drug. He could afford, he thought, to give himself up to it because it had a fixed and foreseeable end. When he was nineteen he would leave for the army. The false security of this undermined his will and kept him dangling. That, and the confusion of his feelings.

He was, in his own way, as much under Fergus's spell as she was; but if he was to have her it could only be at Fergus's expense. And always there was the hopeful, hopeless possibility that she would see at last that her passion for Fergus could have no outcome, and that it was he, who had always loved her and stayed patiently close, practising always a difficult loyalty to both, who was her natural partner.

One day in early autumn, not long before he left at last to go on service, they were returning, all three, from an afternoon's hunting in the woods beyond the Park when Fergus led them, on a dry path along the edge of the bog, towards a row of mean little shacks in a spinney, one-roomed, earth-floored hovels where turf-cutters and their families lived, in an area overgrown with weeds and brambles, with occasionally, in a cleared space, a few late beans on a trellis and a gooseberry bush.

Dirty-faced children, the smallest in nothing but a shirt, played in the mud-puddles beside the path. They stopped and stood staring as Fergus on his giant bay, Virgilia on a little fine-boned chestnut mare that pranced, and he himself, riding a short distance behind on his black, came clattering down the road under the leaves, stirring the dust and making an impromptu display.

Big clouds like overladen haywagons were stalled overhead, their edges bruised purplish-grey, threatening a shower. There was a smell of rain on the air, and in the heaviness of the elders, a breathing towards it. The first of the fallen leaves, disturbed by the horses' hooves, sent up a pungent odour of early mould.

They turned off into the spinney. Fergus sprang down

and lifted the couple of hares he had got from where they hung big-eyed at his saddle-pack.

'Come on,' he said, 'I've a call to make.'

'Here?'

Virgilia, doubtful, her lively little horse cutting sideways and kicking up dust, eyed the row of huts and the children who hung along the willow fence.

'It's all right,' he told her, 'it's quite safe.'

She lifted her chin. 'It isn't that,' she said. 'Who's to look after the horses?'

Fergus made a sign to a couple of big freckled boys of nine or ten who were among the starers.

'Here,' he shouted, 'take the lady's horse.'

He dipped into his pocket for a coin and the older boy turned it in a grubby palm. 'I'll give you another when we get back.' His own horse, which was quiet, he passed to the second boy. When Adair came up a moment later, the second boy ran forward and held it while he swung down.

Fergus, the two hares slung over his wrist, led the way past the first of the roped-thatch huts.

On the flattened weeds in front of it a pasty-faced woman with bristling hair was weaving a basket. Bundles of osier stood against the wall behind her. There was a crib at her feet and two small children, thin and barefooted, clung to her knees.

'What's that you've got?' she called. 'Is it for the O'Riordans?'

He held up the hares.

'Look, Brendan,' she said, and the older of the two children put his head out from behind her skirt, 'look a' the fiadh.'

'Good luck to ye,' she called after them as they made their way on the narrowing path that led into the spinney.

'Fergus,' Virgilia said, 'where are we going?' She was

impatient rather than anxious. He was always playing this game of surprises and secrets.

'You'll see.'

A little barefooted girl appeared before them, who stared a moment, then fled, and they heard her calling ahead.

'It's Fergus, Fergus is come. Mam, Mam, Fergus is here.' She ran back and hung on to his belt.

'Are them for uz?' she asked, crinkling her nose at the hares. She was thin, milk-skinned, with long uncombed black hair.

The hut when they came to it stood behind the remains of an osier fence that had been pushed sideways at one point, perhaps by a runaway pig, and the yard was bare and stalky, with a few dried-out canes still upright in the ground, bearing nothing, and a pile of charred stones among the weeds where a fire had been lit. Two younger children ran out and seemed ready to dance and shout but sobered when they saw Fergus was not alone. They stood, the little girl with a dirty thumb in her mouth and her eyes narrowed, the boy, bolder, looking to Fergus for explanation.

'Hello there,' Fergus said, 'Annie, Declan.'

The children let them pass, Fergus leading, into the dim, strong-smelling interior, and then hung at the door, watching as Fergus introduced them to a shapeless woman with thin hair and no teeth who might have been any age from thirty-five to sixty and a fierce-looking girl of maybe fourteen, Mrs O'Riordan and her daughter Marnie. In a moment the other children had crowded in to have their names formally given.

'Sit down, won't ye, miss,' Mrs O'Riordan said, showing Virgilia a place set in the hearth. What the children called creepies, little low three-legged stools, were produced for Fergus and Adair. Fergus, his long legs almost at his chin, sat beaming.

It was a mean, low-ceilinged place with a daub floor. A single opening that could be covered with a dried sheepskin, which hung from a nail beside it, provided the only window. Wickerwork showed through breaks in the plaster above the hearth, and at the gable wall at the other end a milch-cow was tethered, with an open drain under its tail that ran to a slurry-pit outside. The smoky fire caught in their throats, made their eyes smart.

Mrs O'Riordan explained that the house, by some misfortune, had been built on a fairy path, which accounted for their bad luck but also for the door, which had to be kept open in even the severest weather and the little pitcher of water beside it.

The girl who had met them on the path, and who it appeared was the family look-out, came in now with two older boys of twelve and fifteen, who had been cutting turf in the bog. They were grimed and sweaty, their legs stained to the knee with bog-water. They set their slanes against the wall, and the older of the two, very manly and serious, shook hands with Fergus and then with Adair. The other, who seemed simple-minded, stood gawking. They were all very constrained, but once the hares had been laid in the shallow basket that served as a table, and had been poked at and squirmed over and admired, things went easier. Fergus was already at ease, but soon the children were too, plying him with questions, tugging at his shirt when they wanted to speak, swarming over him like puppies while he laughed and tumbled them off. At last he caught the smallest of them back, settled her on his lap, and began to recreate for them the noise and excitement of the hunt. How the dogs performed, how they had got one hare, then the other.

'Why didn' ye bring the dogs?' the simple boy asked (instead of us, Adair thought, meeting Virgilia's amused eye as she too saw it) and Fergus explained that there were too many of them and that they had a handler to take care of them.

'How many is there?' the boy wanted to know. 'What are they called?'

'Donagh, shh now,' Marnie told him. 'You mustn' keep on askin'.' But Fergus told him. Five, and each of the names.

'Lockie is a good 'un,' the boy said, out of a place in himself that was not quite in the room. Something in the name appealed to him and he laughed, and they all laughed except Marnie, who remained very stern and disapproving and did not for a moment drop her fierceness. She was, Adair saw, ashamed before them, but most of all before Virgilia. Fergus, who had also seen it, tried to draw her out.

'Marnie,' he told them, 'can read a little. I taught her – eh Marnie? And she teaches the others. You can read a little, can't you, Declan?' This to a boy of six or seven who was clinging to his knee. But Marnie was not pleased by this attempt to draw attention to her. All she did was glare. A couple of Burton books in their dirty white covers were brought out and Declan read them a few hair-raising paragraphs from *The Irish Rebels and Rapparees*.

'He's very good to uz,' Mrs O'Riordan told Virgilia. 'I don't know what we'd have done otherwise.'

Fergus shook his head. But the affection they all had for him, and the pleasure he took in it, was too plain to be hidden. 'O'Riordan,' he told them quietly, 'was transported.'

'Seven years,' the woman announced. 'Do you know, sir,' she asked Adair, 'where New South Wales is?'

It was the first he had heard of it. Now, sitting in the dead of night in the very heart of it, he cast his mind back to that afternoon and the woman's question. Somewhere out here, Fergus, all six feet six of him, if it was him, lay a bare three feet under the surface, at a spot unnamed and strange, having run to the ends of the earth not to become

156

what blood at least had intended, the last in that sequence of green mounds at the end of the Walk. How could they have known then, either of them, any of them – for there was also Virgilia – the part it would play in their lives?

New South Wales. When the woman dropped the name into the dead air of the hut, and the children's faces hardened around it – *they* had heard it often enough – he had felt no premonitory stirring in him. It conjured up no point on the globe, no fact or association.

'No,' he told her, 'I do not.'

'Ah,' she said, 'I thought you would have. He has, Fergus has. It's many a poor man has gone there.'

'Here,' Fergus said to break the mood that had come over them, and easing the child on to one knee, he rooted about in his pocket. 'I've brought you something.' He spilled half a dozen walnuts, one for each child, out of his pocket, and the girl who had met them on the path, and regarded herself as a favourite, gathered them up and handed them round. The children immediately sat and began cracking them with their teeth.

'These are for you,' he said, producing two little mandarin oranges, one for Mrs O'Riordan, the other for Marnie, who could not resist a half-secret smile as she pushed hers into the pocket of her apron.

'I'm sorry,' Mrs O'Riordan told them, 'I've no tea nor nothin' I can offer you.'

She set her orange in the rishawn beside the two hares, where no doubt she would divide it out later among the children.

Riding away, Fergus, in an unusually expansive mood, told them of O'Riordan's crime – he had been accused of belonging to a band of sheep-stealers – and of the woman's courage, and the affection and good nature of the children, and how the two older boys, Donagh and Sean, worked fourteen hours a day cutting turf to keep a roof over their heads and to feed them.

The rain, a brief shower, had come and gone while they were in the hut. Rich smells of dust and soaked grass rose up to meet them, mixed with the smell of wet leather and horse. The air, refreshed and cleared of heat, was so sparklingly clear that the whole countryside, as they rode out of the spinney, all drenched and dripping sunlight from every leaf, was laid out before them.

Far off, beyond the peat bog and the woods where Fergus had taken his hares, was the white façade of the Park, picked out with brilliant clarity under a sky that was cloudless now, with just the faint hint in its blue of a rainbow.

Virgilia was silent; impressed, as Adair himself was, by the O'Riordans, but even more by an aspect of Fergus they had not seen till now and could scarcely have imagined. He had been noisy enough with the children, boisterous even, but there was as well a gravity in his dealing with even the youngest of them, as of an older brother or substitute father, that was quite new, as if a side of him that till now he had had no use for had emerged in response to the family's needs, each one of them, but even more to the affection they showed him, which he took in an easy way as the most natural thing in the world.

Their affection, Adair thought, and especially Virgilia's, he took always as if it made demands on him that it was not in his nature to meet. Not because he was not fond of them but because their needs were so exclusive and he was unwilling to be contained. It was this, Adair thought, rather than the looks the older girl, Marnie, had given her, the rivalry, absurd as it might be, for possession, that disturbed Virgilia. Perhaps she had begun to see what he felt he had always known: that it would not be another woman who would occupy his heart and keep his spirit always beyond her reach.

It was clear, or ought to have been, from the exalted mood he was in: which communicated itself to every part of him and from his spirit to theirs, and seemed to glow out of every aspect of the landscape – from the pools in the distance that flashed out where the last of the shower had not yet been sucked into the earth, from the tips of the leaves overhead – and would live in Adair's memory of their ride home as an atmosphere they moved in that Fergus created by his presence at their side, and which he and Virgilia, in their different ways, breathed and fed on but could no more hold than the air itself, or the light that played with such high drama over the Park meadows, making new, unfamiliar, unforgettable, the familiar scene.

He was away for four years on that first tour: serving in small frontier towns in Galicia and the Krajina; writing home regularly, the dutiful son, to Mama Aimée, who did not always reply, and sending long, increasingly expansive and expressive letters to Virgilia in which he began, under the influence of her desire to analyse and question even the smallest nuances of feeling, to examine his own.

In the beginning it was no more than an exercise in pleasing her, in complying, which had become a habit in him, with her exigent demands; but self-analysis, a conscientious probing in himself of hidden motives and desires, of all the devious means by which the heart, but also the mind, indulges and deceives, became a kind of passion in him; no longer simply a way of catching and holding her attention by playing, with a certain degree of masculine cynicism, the part that would most interest her, but of uncovering in himself, and more now for his own sake than for hers, this other and deeper self that sprang into existence when his pen traced the magic words 'My Dear Virgilia' and his soul added, silently, 'My Dearest'.

Isolated as he was among strangers, and in a profession whose daily routine denied him, with its promiscuity and clatter, the retreat into quietness which he now discovered was one of the cravings of his nature, he found in writing to her an escape into the deepest privacy of all, the one a man shares with the blank page, with candle, ink and pen in the deep hours of night, when others, a whole barracks full of men, in their regulation cots and hammocks, lie released from the discipline that makes them equal and uniform into the free world of sleep, into an area, beyond surveillance, where, their clothes laid aside, their skin soaked with moonlight, they can indulge without fear of scrutiny in the most outrageous insubordination, the simplest or most grotesque desires.

What he released himself into was a kind of dreaming-on-the-page; which, insofar as speaking on paper is a speaking across distance to one whose attention can be taken for granted, whose eye reading the not-yet written page one assumes already to be focused and engaged, is a sharing, a deep communion of mouth to ear and soul to soul, such as he could never have contemplated when she was near, and which drew out of him, awkwardly at the beginning, then with increasing boldness, a more eloquent, more perceptive, more passionate self – anatomist, *philosophe*, lover.

He had embarked on a new means of wooing her, and as his changed and changing self crept forth and made itself visible, apprehensible, through the alchemy of language itself, in forms whose boldness, whose grandeur of concept and fantasy surprised even himself, little turns of expression that revealed new views to him of what he thought and felt, he grew full of an elated confidence, and when she

160

responded it was to this new self he had uncovered to her, phrase matching phrase in the same passionate intimacy, and he was ever more powerfully drawn on.

He had suspected her at first of writing only so that she could speak, even in passing, of Fergus; and it was true, there was always some mention of him. And why not? It was news he was always eager to hear. But more and more freely, more openly now, she spoke, in response to the frankness of his own unveilings, of herself.

After four years and so much that had now been stated between them, it worried him, when he decided to go home on leave, how they would meet again as their former selves.

The two figures who had come into being through all this passing back and forth of sheets of paper, however close they came to what was most real in them, existed on a level of language that could not, he thought, be translated into ordinary discourse, and would shrink back, to hover as ghostly onlookers, from a world whose familiar scenes and habits, whose many reminders of previous occasions, old awkwardnesses, and affections, judgements, errors, would inevitably call back their heavier, more ordinary selves, and especially in his case he thought – and in a way that could only disappoint her and rob him, when he saw it, of his new-found assurance – the hot ungainly youth who still haunted his flesh. He would, out of professional habit, swagger a little, even without the dash and glitter of his uniform, and she would look grave and ask herself: is he, after all, so conventional? He would stumble, become tongue-tied. What then of the letters? Did he get someone else to write them? This was all foolishness of course – he was always running away with himself – but there was something of truth in it, and he came, day by day, to dread the moment when he must face her.

He had forgotten how generous she was, and how acutely aware, in her quick way, of contradictions, not least her own.

Six months before, Eamon Fitzgibbon had been struck with a paralysis that had left him entirely without speech. He had a man to attend to his grosser needs, to wash and dress and feed him, but only through Virgilia now could he communicate with the world; it was she who sat with him in the long winter afternoons, to read aloud from his favourite authors, Plutarch and Montaigne, and deciphering with slow patience his attempts to speak.

'Do you remember, Michael,' she said lightly, 'what a determined little fibber I used to be? You warned me then that the world would catch up with me.'

It was his second visit. They had got away, but only for a few moments, and were walking together by the lake.

'Don't,' he said.

A mist lay over the scene, with as always a smell of the sea in it, so that you were aware, even in the molten stillness, of Atlantic breakers and the crying of gulls. Perhaps it was that, he thought, that had led them so often into dreams of distance: the smell of the ocean in their sheets; that side of their world that was always open and on the move, from which all their weather came, mist, slow drizzle, slashing rain-storms that tore the roof-tiles off and uprooted trees, also the days, like this, of dreamy calm.

'Oh, it's all right,' she said. 'I don't mean I have quite given in to the dullest, most absolute truth. But events are events. No amount of wishful thinking will change them.' She gave him one of her affectionate, half-mocking looks. 'When you first came here – how old were you, five? – you were such a sober little body, such a prig. I couldn't believe my luck. I loved seeing how shocked you looked at the whoppers I told. How grave and concerned you were. And how you blushed – for me, no doubt, but also because you knew you were going to let me get away with it. What a dilemma for such a moral little soul. You'd look away and pretend you hadn't heard, but there'd be a little crease on your brow – just there – that you couldn't hide. You were afraid, I think, that I would go to hell and that you were guilty, out of embarrassment, of having failed to save me.'

He felt the edge of defiance in her. If there was much that she had, through circumstances, given up, there was more that she had not. There was a new hardiness about her, a briskness in all her movements, but especially in her walk, that might have less to do, he thought, with her need to get back to her father's side than with an adherence to her dream of travel for which she was secretly in training, a determination not to yield to the enclosed life that for a time was forced upon her and which she had accepted, though it was not in her nature, out of a passionate stoicism that was. She had not relinquished even the least of her ambitions, or her belief, long held, that the only proper exercise of the spirit was in risk.

He visited the Park as often as he could get away, and there was usually the chance of a few minutes together. They talked and were easy, though not as easy as when they wrote, but by some unstated agreement spoke almost never of Fergus, though he was always, Adair thought, the third who walked in company with them, or, lost in his own abstractions, dawdled, as he had so often done, at a distance behind.

In fact these glances over his shoulder at a figure who was not there were the only glimpse he had of Fergus in his first seventy-two hours at home, and he wondered if

163

Fergus was deliberately avoiding him. Then, one morning, on the fourth or fifth day of his leave, he woke to a strangeness in the room that he took at first to be the last glimmerings of a dream that when he presently set his mind to it would come flooding back in all its brilliant detail. But when he sat up on one elbow it was to discover Fergus, already dressed for the outdoors in greatcoat and riding breeches, seated in the low window opposite and regarding him with a look of soft amusement.

'What is it?' he asked. 'What has happened?'

'Nothing. I've come to take you out, that's all.'

'How long have you been there?'

'Three minutes – five? You had such a happy look I didn't like to wake you.'

Adair pushed sideways, pushed down for a moment into the blankets. It was true, he did feel happy. Extravagantly so. Was it the dream he had been having, whose physical exaltation still filled him, and which he felt even more strongly when he yawned and stretched his limbs, or some quality that Fergus had brought into the room, some old affection and intimacy between them that he had the power to restore just by being there, and which, as he rolled out of bed and set his foot down, Adair felt like the return of the easiest and most joyful occasions of their boyhood?

'Don't mind me,' Fergus said.

Adair stood rubbing his skull with the flat of his hand, aware, now that he was out of the warm envelope of the bedclothes and his own body heat, how sharp the air was. The light on the ceiling and all round the figure Fergus made in the long window-frame was bluish.

He clapped his arms to his chest and did a heavy-footed dance on the cold floor. 'Ah,' he said, realizing at last what it was, 'it's been snowing.'

'All night. Get a move on, won't you? We'll miss the best of it if you don't. It's after nine.'

Adair poured water into the bowl on the wash-stand while Fergus held the towel for him, splashed his face and shoulders, quickly pulled on his clothes, and they set off with just a glass of spirits at the stable door while they stood waiting for the horses to be fetched.

The yard was frozen. Great drifts of snow hung from the eaves and occasionally sifted down or fell with a thump. Their breath fumed. Fergus, who was always at his most energetic in such weather, stamped snow from his boots, his cheeks glowed. 'You haven't had a decent outing all week,' he told him. 'You'll enjoy it. You'll see.'

He did. It was like old times. They rode easily together, scarcely speaking but happily in tune, and went round the shanty pubs in out-of-the-way villages, tossing down an inch or two of harsh-tasting poteen that burned in their throat and nostrils but warmed them against the cold, then rode on; in every place they stepped into finding noisy companions who immediately called on Fergus to come and join the smoky huddle they made where they sat with their boots up on the hearth and their coats open to take the heat, and were eager to carry them home to dinner. Rough fellows, most of them, only momentarily intimidated, Adair found, by his self-consciousness, which he lost when they lost theirs in the guarantee that if Fergus knew him he must be a boyo.

At midday they ate potato and sorrel soup with the family of a horse-trader, who spent most of the meal trying to talk Fergus into buying a dappled dark bay they had looked at in a barn at the end of a potato-field where dark haulms stuck up out of the snow and a fierce wind sent the new flakes scurrying.

Somewhere along the way they were joined by a dirty,

drunken boy of about fifteen. He had attached himself to Fergus in one of the most isolated of the shebeens they visited at the end of a lough, where a toothless old granny doled out burning liquor to a lot of tinkers and their women while a youth played jigs on a fiddle, though most of the company was too drunk to dance. When they-left, the boy had run along barefoot beside them till Fergus took him up behind, and he was with them for a couple of hours, angelfaced, incoherent, occasionally trying to kiss Fergus's neck or put his hand into his shirt. But in another place, further on, he passed out, and they left him with a group of tramps who knew him – Butty, he was called – and settled him to sleep it off by the hearth.

Later they ate again in a hut on the outskirts of another village, in a room where twenty pigeons moaned and gurgled behind a willow enclosure against the wall. Other birds danced about in osier cages of every shape that hung from the ceiling, and threw strange shadows against the light of the cruisie lamps; including a blackbird that would burst without warning into exuberant song, and in another cage a jackdaw that every ten minutes or so interrupted the lively talk around the hearth with shouts of 'Take care, Jack!', at which one of the children would get up and push a bit of crust through the bars so that the daw said 'Thankee, and good luck.'

The whole family was involved in bird-trapping and bird-trading. One of the younger boys explained to Adair that they trapped every sort of bird except the swallow and the robin. 'For every swallow, you know, sir, has three drops o' the devil's blood in it – no man I know'd ever touch one – and the robin is a blessed bird. If I find a robin in me crib, sir, I put a bit o' printed paper in its mouth an' I say, "Spiddogue, spiddogue, now swear on this book in your mouth to send next time a thrush or a blackbird into me crib." Then I pull out his tail-feather for a token, to know 'im again, and that's how it's done, sir.'

In each of these households Fergus was welcomed as one of the family and in this last, since it was after ten and the snow was falling again, they were urged to stay.

'Should we?' Fergus demanded.

The children clamoured and yelled, 'Yes Fergus, do, do.'

'Would you like that, Michael?' he asked. 'To stay here and sleep in shadogue? They won't mind, I often do it.'

Adair was tempted. The house was warm and jolly, in spite of the strong smell of fish oil from the lamps, and he did not want to break the long day's intimacy between them and the happiness that all day, since the moment he woke and found Fergus there in the window watching over the last moments of his sleep, had never left him. He had ridden, for all the bitter weather, wrapped in the intense warmth of it.

(Now, after so long, he felt it again, and so powerfully that he could not believe it would not communicate itself in the darkness to Daniel Carney, and he waited to hear him, at any moment, speak out of his own recollection of the man he had known as Dolan, out of a sense of his immediate warmth and presence beside them. He would have then, at least to the satisfaction of his own mind, and as much as he would ever have, his proof. He heard Carney shift in the dark, disturbed out of half-sleep, but no word came from him.)

They had slept on fresh rushes and bundles of woollen breadeen.

'You'll not feel the cold, you know,' the woman of the house told them, 'on a bed o' rushes. Our Lord himself slept on one. So did the Fianna. It'll get your strength up.'

The cages of the song-birds were covered with shawls and old clouts, but all night he was half aware of the pigeons settling and unsettling, scraping their feet in the dark, and had woken once to scratch a bite, not knowing for a moment where he was and alarmed by the strange shapes in the air above him, which seemed alive, but was soothed by the breathing all round of other sleepers, and the snuffling close by of one of the children, and soon sank back into his own world of sleep. Only when he woke to the stooped shape of one of the women restocking the fire and the birds cawing and gargling, and lay still a moment settling himself back into his skin, did he recall that when he woke in the night Fergus had no longer been beside him, though he was there again now, with his greatcoat round his shoulders and his long legs drawn up. He wondered, as they sat sipping the warm, rather salty milk from the keeler, which of the women of the household he had crept away to. There was no telling from the closed, friendly faces.

But their outing was not repeated, and was, he guessed, a thing Fergus had arranged specially to make up for the fact that they were otherwise to see so little of one another.

He spent some time each day listening to Mama Aimée, whose complaints now had become ritualized into a formula that was endlessly repeatable, so that his chief preoccupation as they sat drinking chocolate in her little sitting-room, or visiting, as she still loved to do, her horses, was to avoid the cues that set her off, and when she did begin, to lead her as subtly as possible to another subject.

She could sometimes be tempted, these days, to speak of her youth, and for the first time, in her reminiscences of midnight feasts at Miss Bonnifer's Academy in Dublin, and the pranks some of the young ladies got up to on their excursions to the sea at Howth, he caught a glimpse of a lively figure at her side who was his mother, but too late for him to form, as he might have done twenty years before, any clear image from it.

The girl Mama Aimée evoked was wayward enough, and already scandalously in communion with the young man who would become his father, a local tenor much frequented by Miss Bonnifer's young ladies, who were all in love with him; he had just begun to make a reputation for himself in concert halls and at the theatre.

But the stories Mama Aimée had to tell were the merest sketches. She had reduced them over the years to conventional tales of girlish high spirits and innocent indiscretions, with no details to catch the imagination or the heart. However bright a picture they might make in her own memory, the two friends she spoke of, for all their closeness and the many little confidences and promises for the future they exchanged, remained for him too far-off, too shadowy, even with the evidence of Mama Aimée before him, to become flesh and blood. He wondered why she had waited so long to tell what might, twenty years before, have meant so much to him, and he felt a terrible pity for the child he had been and whose heart he could still feel, in a quite disconcerting way, beating painfully in his breast, who had been so conscious of having come here with nothing of his own, no memories, no ties, only the ones he must make in this new life he had been given. He felt again a little of that child's panicky bewilderment and was astonished at his courage, at the mixture of opportunism and stubborn will that had allowed him to survive, and felt a kind of anger, even now, at the anxiety he had suffered, which he thought had shaped more of his present nature than he dared acknowledge.

And after all that, it was he and Mama Aimée who sat together here; he listening more patiently than any son, more patiently, certainly, than Fergus, to the long rigmarole of a life she saw only in terms of its losses; she playing more intimately than ever now the part of the mother he had never known. Is that why she had made so little effort in the old days to make his lost mother real to him? To make certain that his ties of affection would be only to her? To make certain that he would be here, twenty years later, when she would most have need of him, to sit through a long winter's morning while she evoked the light-headed, careless creature who had given him birth, and her friend, the big older girl whose plainness and good sense his mother might have taken as a balance to her own dangerous lightness, and who would provide, when the time came, the bread and butter that would save her orphaned child from destitution.

Long views, long views . . .

But there was another thought that occurred to him. It was this: that he had somehow, innocently, unwittingly, stolen Fergus's birthright. That part of Mama Aimée's failure to accept Fergus was because she had already given her heart to him, and that when he gave his, and so completely, to the other child, she had, also innocently, unwittingly, turned against the boy. Unreasonable, unnatural? It might seem so, but he had long since given up the belief that the forces that move us have anything to do either with nature or reason, or that the heart moves in anything but the most crooked way.

But this image of himself as cuckoo, which was a new one and which he thought threw his whole relationship with Fergus into a new light, was disturbing to him. If Fergus had forgiven Mama Aimée, surely he must. But could he forgive himself? Had he really, for all his devotion to the boy, innocently, unwittingly – and why did he insist on these terms, what did they mean? – replaced Fergus in his mother's heart?

*

Each morning, when he had done his duty to Mama Aimée, he rode across to the Park.

His way to Virgilia would be barred on most occasions by Marnie O'Riordan, whom Virgilia, at Fergus's urging, had taken on as her maid. Very prim, and with a tart, disapproving manner that went oddly with her youth, she appeared to regard all visitors to the Park, however familiar, as intruders.

Adair was puzzled by her hostility towards him and believed at first that it must be out of loyalty to Fergus; that she regarded him as a rival to Fergus in Virgilia's affections and meant, with a bluntness that had its comic side it was so obvious, to keep him off. But he saw after a time that she was acting on her own behalf. The keynote of her nature was a fierce possessiveness. Having transferred to Virgilia the proprietorial affection she had shown, on the day of their visit, for Fergus, she resented the few minutes each day that he and Virgilia found to walk by the lake; even more, that he was admitted as an equal to the hours she spent with her father in the dim library, a place Marnie appeared to regard as the one area in the house that was entirely closed to her, not by actual prohibition but, like some dark cave in a fairy-tale, by the spirits that hovered around its entrance and governed the obscure hocus-pocus through which Virgilia and her father managed their silent conversation.

'What a terrier she is.' He laughed. 'I feel I ought to turn up with a bag of currant buns to throw at her. If she had her way I'd never see you at all.'

'No,' Virgilia told him, 'it's just her way. Of insisting on her place here. That she's important to me. In fact she's quite fond of you.'

'She disguises it well enough.'

'She has her dignity to protect. She remembers the conditions under which you first saw her. But her fierceness is all show. Give her a little affection and she's a perfect lamb.'

In the Library, while Eamon Fitzgibbon waited impatiently in his chair, he watched her lay out on the green baize table-top the counters of their 'talk'.

Unlike Marnie, he felt more at home in this room than anywhere else in the Park. So much of what was most passionate in him had had its first stirrings here, so much of what he knew was shut up safe in the books round its walls, or hovering in the air in dusty whispers not yet stilled. It was also the place where he felt closest to *her*.

Certain spaces, with their shadows and secrecies, seem inevitably associated in our minds with particular forms of feeling, so much so that we think of them as their perfect counterpart; if they were different, if the light that filled them had a different quality, or fell at a different angle, what we feel would be different; or so it seems. And so it was, for him, in the Library. Even the memory of it, of its particular dimensions, the way the light, at its dim edges, touched the gilt spines of the volumes along a wall, like the entrance there to a mysterious wood, could evoke in him a mood in which she was immediately and substantially present, as she was now, her back bent, her pale fingers sorting the letters that had been traced on wooden blocks.

Turning them upwards, she arranged them in broken lines.

When they were ready she took a little ivory stick and pointed to each one in turn while the old man nodded or furiously shook his head.

Slowly, painfully, the words appeared that constituted a conversation between them.

Looking on, Adair was surprised, moved too, by the

patience she showed, but the tension in the room was terrible. The gestures involved were so small, and he had thought of them both, father and daughter, as having spirits that ranged over large tracts of time and space – to ancient Rome and back, in Eamon's case, with a large-minded ease and eagle grasp of illimitable vistas; even further perhaps in her case, into spaces not yet named or imagined, though they might, for practical purposes, go under the code-name of desert or equatorial forest.

He watched her point now to a single letter and have it rejected. To another, trying to guess where his mind was moving. Rejected again.

The old man, whose quickness of intellect and wit was quite unimpaired, clenched his fist and his brow, worked his throat in a hopeless effort to suggest the letter he intended. The veins stood out on his brow. The skull with its grizzled hair was bursting.

And Virgilia, holding in her own impetuous spirit, sat slowing her pulse – he could feel it – steeling her nerves, submitting herself to this snail's pace at which they lumbered across the afternoon dragging behind them letter after letter, word after word, to make the cryptic messages laid out between them, nouns, verbs, for which, as she wrote them down on a pad, she had to supply by trial and error the teasing connectives.

'You should rest,' Adair told her. 'Let me do this. I can do it. Can't I, Eamon?' and he laid his hand affectionately on the old man's sleeve.

'No,' she told him. 'I must. It's all right, I'm not tired. It's all right, Pa,' she told her father, who was alarmed but also, Adair saw, ashamed, 'I'm not going anywhere.'

Later, when they went out to walk a little in the snowy park, she explained. 'Of course you could do it, Michael, anyone could. And he's fond of you – there's no one he loves more. But it's me he needs to keep – talking to. It's like the tiniest tiniest air-hole that he's breathing through. If it wasn't there he'd have no will to live. I'm the one who has to be on the other side of it. But you can help me read to him, he'd like that. We'll take turns.'

So it was, once again after so long, like their earliest days in this room. They read in turn, one or two pages at a time, but not haltingly now, from the lives of Numa and Cato and Lucullus, stern masters of Roman virtues, and something in these texts that had shaped them both shone again with the force of revelation, renewed in them an old reciprocal understanding, so that this reading back and forth, tuning their ear to the timbre of the other's voice, listening for the note of affirmation or mature scepticism or late recognition of an irony they had formerly missed, became another form of correspondence and they felt closer in these hours, with the silent but watchful presence in the winged chair opposite and a man who had been dead for nearly eighteen hundred years to find the words for them, than when they slipped out to take in the invigorating air, or in those briefer moments when she came down herself to help him into his coat and kissed him, in a sisterly way, at the door.

9

HE SLEPT AGAIN, and this time what he dreamed he did remember.

He was standing in clear sunlight at the edge of a vast sheet of water, so dazzling with salt and reflected light that he could not see the farther shore and had for a moment to shield his eyes against its blinding throb. He was aware of another presence, close at his side but slightly behind. He felt its heaviness there, but knew he must not turn his head to look or it would vanish, and with it the lake or inland sea and its wash of light, and he too, since he understood that the figure there at his side was himself, a more obscure, endangered self with a history that was his but had somehow been kept secret from him. The tenderness and concern he felt was for both of them.

He knew this country well enough by now to be sceptical of his senses. The lake, with the next step he took, could quite easily shrivel up with a cackle, and there would be in its place only an equally vast expanse of sharp and dazzling stones. Meanwhile, mirage or not, he held it. I have to take the risk, he told himself, and the figure at his side granted assent.

He took a step. The vision held. The great sheet of light exulted, all ripples.

Another.

Again it shivered, shook out lines of light, and he saw now that sea-birds were brooding in the furrows, gulls, and that other birds, waders on long stilts, were either stilled in the shallows or walking in a stately manner, one clawed foot raised, held, then solemnly lowered, in a parade along the shore. Fish heaved in shoals below its smooth and polished surface, great swathes of shadow that suddenly showed silver where their backs broke water and their scales caught the sun. Such plenty!

It is real, he breathed. It is a door in the darkness, a way out. His heart lifted at the thought and there came a clatter, far out, an explosion of wings, and he saw that in the midst of the commotion was a boat, a low dug-out driven by many rowers; far out but rapidly approaching. He stepped forward to call to them. But the moment his breath flew out there was an answering upheaval, as if a sudden wind had struck the lake. Its surface rippled like silk, and the whole weight and light of it was sucked upwards in a single movement that took his breath away; a single, shiningly transparent sack, it was being hauled upwards, as in a theatre, by invisible hands. He tried to shout but was breathless. He reached up, with a terrible tightening of his chest, to pluck it back.

It was moving fast now, like an air-balloon, soaring aloft till it was just a distant, spherical drop, rather milky; then, as the sun struck it, a brilliant speck. Gone, with all its vision, of light, birds, fish, men, rescue. He was choking. At the end of his breath. But the presence at his side was still there, breath labouring, pumping.

He woke, and had the uneasy feeling of having stepped from one dream into another that was even more remote. He laboured to catch his breath. Daniel Carney's one eye was fixed upon him with a savage watchfulness.

'I must have dozed off,' he said. It was half a question.

'Yes sir, you did sleep for a bit.'

'How long?'

'A minute or two. Maybe less.'

A minute or two? Had he really experienced so much in so short a time? Could the mind – out of what rich well? – draw up such bright, such enlarging images, play so powerfully on the nerves, hold out the promise of hopeful issue, of escape from the hard facts of circumstance, only so that some natural or supernatural force could pluck it away again, and all this in the space of a hundred tumultuous heart-beats?

As on many occasions before, he was struck by the difference between minutes as the watch in his pocket might have ticked them off and this other time he carried in his head, which was infinitely expandable and had nothing to do with the movements of either the earth or the sun.

Again he was aware of Carney's gaze upon him, intense, almost predatory, as if he might have news to bring him out of what he had dreamed. News of rescue, was it? Could he know that? Of a rescue that at the last moment had failed? He felt a kind of warning that he should control his thoughts if he did not want them known; that the space they shared was no longer a contained one with fixed walls and a roof, but was open, and in such a way that the normal rules of separation, of one thing being distinct to itself and closed against another, no longer applied.

I am not properly awake, he thought. I was right the first time. I have wakened into another dream.

My dear Virgilia, he began writing in his head, my dear, my dearest . . .

'It must be nearly dawn,' Carney said.

It was. He saw it now. A faint greyness showed through the cracks in the door and was breaking in through gaps in the walls.

But there was nothing of fear in the man's voice. The hollow note was resignation, a patience of long habit brought now to its last test, acceptance that what his breath, his life was tied to was the inexorable rolling of great stones about the sky. Adair found himself struck with despondency. He had not thought he would feel such dread of the moment when he must say, It is time, I think. What *had* he thought? That the announcement would come from some impersonal voice out of the air?

Despondency – that is what this feeling was called. Darker than dejection. A sense of impotence before the powers.

There were days, waking here to the peppery scent of unfamiliar dust, and an air sick, already exhausted, loaded with heat, when, in a depression of spirit in which his moral fibre and all his nerves were worried and frayed, he felt the hopelessness, the absurdity of his endeavours and of all that had brought him half-way round the world to this impossible country.

In such moments it came to him that he would never, in the sense he had intended, reach Virgilia's heart. She would grow old in the fanaticism of her first love. The languor and excited anguish it caused her would become in time – he knew only too well this particular adjustment – its own satisfaction, bitter but also reassuring. She would cling to what she had lost for no other reason than to prove that she had once possessed it, turn devotion into a cult. Though it was on her urging that he had come, would she forgive him for being the bearer to her of the news that Fergus was dead, buried somewhere, under an outlaw's name, in the wastes of this country? Would she believe it? After all, what proof did he have, unless he went out with the black Jonas to find, in all that burning space out there, the shallow ditch with its bones. And whose bones? By what criteria could he ever, with certainty, identify them? And suppose he did, and she accepted at last that Fergus was dead. Would she welcome him into the empty place in her heart? Mightn't

178

the very reminder of Fergus and her loss make his presence intolerable to her?

There were times when, out of despair, he was tempted to stay rather than go back and face her. The sons and daughters he dreamed of, who were her children too, would turn their faces from him, step back into the dark. The seed in his loins would sizzle and dry up. Life here, with its desperate routine and sparse amenities, its brutal pleasures, might come in time to seem normal to him. Every shift of the light would search his soul and ask mockingly, Are you still here then, Michael Adair, Michael Adair? Have you decided after all not to escape?

All this was exaggeration and melancholic fancy; he knew that, but when a certain mood of sick self-pity was on him he could not resist the torment as, turn after turn, he himself applied the screw.

He *did* have an imagination after all, he had Virgilia to thank for that. It was she who had forced into existence this unlikely faculty in him, leading him, as he blindly stumbled in search of her, through romances where he had hoped to learn the language of feeling in her, as well as the secrets of her heart, and had found instead a language for his own. Had found too in the intertwining of their lives – his life with hers, both their lives with that of a present but absent Fergus – a configuration he recognized as belonging to fiction, melodrama, opera; once it was allowed to play over the mess that was ordinary living, it was part of the mind's delight in its own ingenuity to find some deep conformity between the shape of story and the shape of dreams.

But his nature was in the end too robust not to reject such grim imaginings. He turned back at last, with deepening breath, to what was restoratively healthy in him.

'Perhaps,' he wrote, 'you could get the terrible Marnie to put in a word for me.'

He said this jokingly, but meant it too. He felt he had at last earned some credit in that quarter. It was Marnie who had first brought them news that Fergus might be in New South Wales. It had come from her father, who thought he had seen him there. A fellow like that, how could he miss him? Was there another such? So it was Marnie, for whom assurance, once she got hold of a thing, was like second sight, not to be challenged with disbelief, who had stepped forward and, in a pleated bonnet in which her pinched little face was lost, stood at the gate to usher him through into the underworld.

The image pleased him. It was sufficiently absurd. He had had a vision of them then – he, Virgilia, Fergus – as figures in a melodrama he had already seen in a dozen forms in the half-light of a dozen smoky theatres, and had laughed at, though as soon as the music struck up he had shivered and was caught. He and Fergus would have their encounter at last on some rocky promontory at the world's end while the band in the pit thumped and sawed and the whole house held its breath.

Well, it hadn't been like that. Still, he had good hopes of Marnie. 'See if that flinty heart,' he wrote, 'has not relented enough to speak a word or two in a poor man's favour.'

He had set out only half-believing he might find some trace of Fergus in the colony, tracking from one place to another the rumour of a tall fellow who did and did not fit his description, this Dolan who had cut such a swathe through the small community, gathering about him as he went the sort of improbable attributes and events that made him, even before he had been shovelled underground, a figure created half out of legend to fulfil the demands of some for a breakaway hero, of others for an embodiment of that spirit of obduracy or malign intent that sets some men defiantly above the law, and wearing so many rags of lurid romanticism that every aspect of the man himself had been lost. What he was after was some shred of proof: some bit of cloth out of a sleeve, it might be, whose texture you could feel between thumb and finger, whose stitches might be recognized as the work of a particular hand; a few words that in themselves provided a signature; a phrase that was the remnant of a secret language, the last echo of a joke made so long ago that it was no more now than an empty habit of speech.

But he had found nothing. Only the conviction that in coming close to Daniel Carney he had at moments been close to Fergus, that the shadow that stepped between them had been his, so near that he could hear in the gap between Carney's breath and his own an easy breathing he knew from many nights at home or by a camp-fire on Ben Breen, and so materially present that he could smell him, if shadows can be smelled and ghosts retain some essence of their former heat and sweat. But what was there to tell in any of that? What was there to show? Mere feeling, mere intimations that know no proof. An emotion he had caught perhaps from the other, and so strongly that he believed he saw what Carney saw; but were the two apparitions identical? A coincidence of feeling – again, feeling – which was gone in a moment and which, quite soon now, only he would be left to recall.

And suppose he did find his clutch of bones. Would they know for certain, either of them, the fingerbones of his hand, the roundness, under the fleshpads of their fingers, of his skull? What would he – what would she – have to go on but again feeling, the same that he had now.

What he had experienced here in the hut was more substantial than that – a shadow, thrown on the heart, of what was as alive in his senses as anything he had ever known, as alive as the man hunched opposite who would himself, in less than an hour now, be a ghost, but till then was still wrapped in the warmth of body-heat and that smell, that was, Adair thought, no more the smell of the soiled and unwashed body, but of life itself.

Proof? There was none. The emptiness of his hand, the fullness of his heart – that was the proof. To accept it she would have to trust him and acknowledge both. If she accepted the second, then the first would not matter, there would be no need of proof, because the power of what his heart had known and held would be more precious to her than the certainty that her old love was dead.

My dear Virgilia, my dear, my dearest . . . let me recommend to you my best quality, since I have at last discovered its name: durability, the durability – I am unabashed by the comparison – of old pewter, old timber – old bones too, I want to say; Paddy's for instance, or mine in the end, for I have a vision before me of years, of a life wonderfully extended. Durability does not shine or flash out. It goes about its daily business of being useful and itself, and for that reason, necessary. This fellow here, this Daniel Carney, whom you do not know, my dearest, and might not at first appreciate – he is crude enough – he has it, we are alike in that, though unlike in so many other ways; and what it constitutes in him, as I see because it has been forced upon me, is a kind of dignity; of beauty too. He is durable, he has proved that; he is here, and would go on being if it was up to him – he has spirit enough; but will not be permitted, I do not know by what law – Well yes, I do. By *our* law, the law of the land, of the world we have made. I mean, I do not know by what larger law. For I confess, privately, to you only my darling, that this lesser law I do not and cannot accept. What is it worth, if all it achieves is the breaking of a man in good health who might, if the world were kinder and more just, be of some use to it, and whose dignity, I do believe, is the equal of those who have judged and will deprive him, in an hour from now, of his one unconditional right in the world, breath, and the full span of what his rude health must decree as 'natural'?– Virgilia, I love these old, durable, worn and useful things, of no particular beauty. But you see it is my own case I am pleading. Isn't that what we argue, each of us, just by being what we are? – As for his case, Daniel Carney's I mean, which is hopeless, I know only that in a world where there is no justice the thing we must cling to above all else is pity if we are to retain some semblance of what makes us men.

But to return to my own case, which means to you, my dearest, always to you. What you have that I do not is that flamey quality, that fierce determination to burn and burn up, that I have had so often to shield my eyes from; I fear it, my soul fears it. I have known this for as long as I can remember. As a boy of six or seven, when I was dazzled, then afraid, what I saw always when I lowered my eyes was the round toes of my boots, and I thought, there is dirt under my feet, and I longed to be outside in the fields where the sky was cast down in sheets in the furrows, hiding its light between them, or in the bog with its buried secrets, old spongy tree-trunks, deep-sunken and secret, which was the world I felt closest to and which would not deny me. But I knew that the moment I was there I would miss the fire, as if all the warmth my body contained was in you. I cannot live without her, I cannot endure – that is what I would tell myself. Well, I have lived without you but I would not have chosen to do so, and I do not now. We must be able at last to look at one another; I to endure the fierceness of your flame, you to endure the dull earth. My dear, my dearest, I say this now because I feel very close tonight to the fact of extinction – not my own, not yet – that will have its hour and I will face that too – but the fact of extinction itself, as real and palpable, as much a part of things, as a drop of moisture on a damp wall, a button, a bowl of porridge. I feel very close to the cold edge of it, because I am close to *him*. No, not Fergus after all, whom I had hoped in one form or another to find here, but this stranger whose animal presence comes near to stifling me, I can smell so strongly the fearsome stink of his body, have in my ear his groans, the wet snuffling of the mucus in his nose, and in a bucket just feet away the foul voiding of his bowels. – There is nothing shameful in this, and little, after so long, that I find offensive.

I had hoped to find some shadow or breath of Fergus here – that is what I came for. But he has been forced into second place in my mind by this other, who has no part in my life but does, after all, mean something to me. Were I to follow my own inclinations I would have him escape, and, because I know already that I shall not, feel a kind of shame, though he has of course no expectation of it, and why should he? – men do not do such things. But why? I ask myself – a childish question – why don't we do them? Are we not free? We are not, but why aren't we? – I know you cannot answer this question, but since you are here I ask it of you just the same and long for your reply. It is the kind of question, when I was a child, I used to put to Eamon. 'I cannot answer these things,' he would tell me. 'I am not God. Ask the priest,' and his voice would take on that mocking tone he always used when he spoke of the Faith, and which made me at times so uncomfortable, 'when you go trotting off next Sunday to Mass.' I think sometimes that he was a spoiled priest, Eamon, but of a religion we have not yet conceived or dared to imagine, and that you, my dear, my dearest, are its priestess and keeper of its flame.

Are they too fierce, the truths of that religion, for us to bear? Can they be more savage than the ones we live with already? I ask this, and though you are here, do not expect an answer . . .

He was drawn back into the hut by a closer voice.

'I reckon, sir, it must be about time.' Little points of light were showing where moisture gathered in the cracks between the slabs.

With lumbering difficulty, Carney began to get to his feet and for the first time Adair saw him upright. He was taller than he had thought, heavier too when he loomed over him, but what Adair was chiefly aware of was not the man's weight or bulk but the grace that had saved him from having to announce the moment himself. He too got to his feet, and lifting the door aside, swung it open on cold air and the wash of first light over the frosty earth.

10

I<small>N THE SILVERY</small> gleam of six o'clock, Kersey, on a bank
above the stream, boots off, jacket unbuttoned, was all
set for a spot of fishing.

He had been out earlier and picked a dozen pint-sized
grasshoppers from the drenched bushes. They were easy to
catch. He talked to each one of them personally; it was a
way, out here, of keeping at a distance the sense you got
that if you didn't make each thing you had to deal with –
a bit of fishing line, a cricket, the pan you were scrubbing,
the cinch you had to buckle – a thing you could draw in
on the line of your breath, then the loneliness and vast
spaces and silence would simply swallow you. 'Com' on,
now,' he whispered, peering in where a fat little hopper,
sticky with dew, sat asleep on a twig. 'You're a lucky feller.
You're in for a big adventure. Sit still, now.'

He reached his hand in, pinched the wings between thumb
and forefinger and slipped the panicky creature into his bag.

Silver perch, that's what he was after. Four he would
need, three if they were fat enough. He had already prepared
a bed of wet brush where they would lie till it was time for
cooking.

When it was over at last, this paddy business, they would
sit quiet for an hour or so and have a good feed before
leaving.

Long trails of mist swathed the trees, there was a dampness on the air. But the sun was coming and would soon

burn it off, it was already lighting the highest leaves. Squatting, he dabbled the tips of his fingers in the creek, shook the cold drops off, and just wetted his mouth and eyes. From that position, almost on a level with the surface of it, he surveyed the stream.

There were three channels. The nearest was shallow and still, a chalky colour, the middle one running; not fast exactly, but enough to ruffle the grey-blue light upon it. The far channel, wider, deeper, was also moving but in a sluggish way. That's where the fish would be. It was overhung by thin-leaved, drooping boughs and was mud-coloured.

He waded out into the middle channel till the water was almost to his knees, steadied himself on the pebbly bottom, and quickly, deftly, at home in a competence, sent the line lancing out.

'Here goes,' he thought.

It fell just where he had intended. 'Com' on, Number One,' he said aloud. 'It's bloody freezing in here, don't keep me waitin'.' His mind went still. A part of him out there under the brownish surface was hanging, waiting. This is more like it, he thought.

He wasn't happy in this outfit, it wasn't what he had expected, it disappointed him. Too old for it, maybe. You needed to be young and not plagued, as he was, by physical troubles that in order to keep up with the others he had to hide, keep to himself.

What irked him was that he wasn't appreciated. He did things for them – Langhurst, for instance. Took extra trouble, put himself out. Did they notice? And the rot they talked! Always going at one another, all so full of chatter and the need to make a test of everything, push, push, push. What pleased him about his present occupation, aside from the fact that you could be on your own for a bit, was that you couldn't push. It was out of your hands. You stayed still. You waited on *his* time, Number One, the old-man perch out there, somewhere in the murky water under the trees, that was hanging, watching, considering, approaching the bait. Responding to the slightest jerking of your forefinger on the line, where you and the breeze just slightly moved it as if it was a live thing. The creature, its gills working, its tail just slightly in motion, hovering out there.

A strike! The force of it, as close and taut as the muscle of his forearm. His mind stopped drifting – it too tensed and plunged. His toes gripped the pebbles underfoot. The fish broke surface, flashed its scales at the sun.

Beautiful, he thought. Swiftly now he began to haul it in.

'You're a real beauty,' he said aloud as his hand closed upon it and with the fingers of the other, he detached the hook, the fish all this while, its power alive and single all down the backbone, jerking in his hand.

'There you are, my beauty,' he said.

He laid it tenderly on the bed of brush. Its rounded eye, still clear, stared straight up into the sky.

'I hoped it'd be you,' he whispered. 'Just you lie there now, don't be nervous. You won't be lonely, I promise. Not for long.'

He stood regarding it with deep satisfaction. It made up for a great deal. It had been just a shadow in his mind, hanging, feeding, a hope; and now here it was out in the open, plump and beautiful, two and a half pounds maybe, its pretty scales all silvery, throwing colours in the sun. His blood beat with the beating of its gills. His raw heart lifted.

A good sign, a good day's beginning.

Number One.

Not far off, under some sparsely foliaged gums away from the creek, Langhurst and Garrety, stripped of their vests and already sweating, were at work on a grave. They had only one shovel between them, so one dug, grunting as he chopped at the loose soil, which immediately sifted back into the hole, while the other, hunkered down on the heel of his boot, complained, offered advice, gave mild instructions.

The sun was up. The feathery leaves overhead moved and flickered, cast a net of shadows over the sandy ground, kept up a continuous shushing sound against the chop chop of the shovel going in and the charged explosions of air as the digger put all the force of shoulders, arm, wrist into getting the thing done as soon as possible.

Langhurst, who for the moment was in the observing position, watched his companion go at it with short sharp strokes, tossing each shovelful over his right arm – he was left-handed – the sinews knotting in his shoulders and his lean neck. Drew his hand across his brow, which was dripping. Blew sweat from his upper lip.

'At least four feet 'e said,' Langhurst told him. 'You still got a way to go.'

'I know that!'

Garrety, fiercely, went back to digging, his eyes hard. As if, Langhurst decided, he was digging his way out of something and his life depended on it. He does everything like that, he thought.

'The blacks 'a got the right idea,' he said. 'You don't catch them workin' their guts out diggin' holes. They wrap 'em up and stow 'em in a tree where the dogs can't get 'em. Less effort all round.'

Garrety grunted and dug. The sand flew.

'I reckon that'll about do,' he said after a time. He panted, rested long-bodied on the handle of the shovel.

Langhurst got to his feet.

'Y' reckon? He's a big bugger. Is it long enough?'

Garrety threw the shovel out and to Langhurst's amazement

laid his long frame on the sandy earth down there, stretched right out with his arms extended, his eyes closed and said, 'See?'

Langhurst, standing just at the lip of the hole, had a dizzy sense of looking down at him from a great height, as if he had shot up higher, much higher, than his five foot ten, or the hole had got deeper. Garrety lay with his eyes closed, hands extended, every bone in his rib-cage visible above the concave belly. The toes of his boots pointed upwards. His cheekbones stuck out where the flesh below them hollowed in the beginnings of a smile.

Langhurst giggled, sat back down on his heels. But when, after a little, Garrety still did not stir but just lay there as if he had dozed off and intended to rest like that for as long as it pleased him, he stood again and noisily cleared his throat.

He felt a little chill at the base of his spine.

Once you stopped moving about and the sweat cooled on your skin it was cold.

He reached for his vest and pulled it over his head. Still Garrety lay.

He couldn't have lain there like that, he felt. So relaxed. In another man's grave.

The light foliage overhead stirred and shifted. The sunlight shifted on Garrety's face. His skin gleamed. There was a shine to it.

A fly settled at the corner of his mouth, and without opening his eyes he brought a hand up and brushed it off. The fly, drunk on sweat, persisted. Suddenly, the long body flexed, shot up, and he was out.

Langhurst found he had been holding his breath. He hadn't noticed it. Kicking the shovel out of the way, Garrety reached down and scooped up his vest. When he raised his arms and drew it over his head, Langhurst could smell him. All his movements, Langhurst thought, had an extra swing to them. As if that moment of complete relaxation down

190

there had replenished something in him. As if, by lying four feet below ground like that and giving himself up to whatever force it was that held you to the earth, he had discovered a source of refreshment, the power to spring to his feet and shoot straight upwards, to stride about filling the place with his musky scent, all easy and light.

He himself felt a sudden heaviness on him that their work here had failed to sweat off, the lingering shadow of a place he had gone to in his dreamless sleep and could not recall, though his belly did.

We're so different, he thought. Me and him.

'God,' Garrety said, turning his face in profile, and from the tenseness of it you might have thought he was in pain. You could see the bunched muscle in his lean jaw, the adam's apple raised then falling, the tendons at work in his neck. 'I can't wait t' get back to town. I'm that randy I could fuck a knot-hole in a bloody wall.'

Four years later, on a clear summer evening two hundred miles to the east of here, Ben Langhurst, with his eighteen-month-old daughter on his arm, behind him a stretch of cleared scrub planted with waist-high apple trees, and his wife, in front of their hut, taking in a line of washing and looking anxiously towards the mounted stranger who had called him to the fence, would hear that his one-time friend, Tom Garrety, after a spell of running in the Ranges with a gang very like the one they had just hunted down, had been shot and killed. The stranger would sit there, watching a little too closely his reaction to the news.

What could he say? With the child still in his arms he would be back at this moment in the shifting light of the gums – four years is not a long step – and the scratching of their bark as the long strips rubbed in the breeze.

191

He would come again to the lip of the grave they had dug together, though it was Garrety who had done most of the work, and see him laid out down there, the gleam of sweat and sunlight in the hollow of his chest and on the prominent cheekbones, his eyelids lowered, at the corner of his mouth a little smile as at a joke known only to himself; and would watch him once again spring to his feet, hanging there on his elongated frame, then rising.

Looking back, he would believe when he went over it again, sitting up alone at a table in the dark and pondering the mystery of their lives, Garrety's, his own which was tied so intimately to the anxious face of the woman in the bed behind him, the rising and falling of a little girl's breath, that what he had seen at that moment was an image out of Garrety's afterlife, and that Garrety in their time together had already had foreknowledge of it, as he had so often, in his uncanny way, known the country up ahead that they were riding into – had known of the reversal his life con-tained, the crossing he would make, had maybe already made, from one side to the other of the law, and it was that that had all along been his secret and the source of his ironic humour. 'You look,' the newsbearer had said, 'as if it didn't too much surprise you.' But he had turned away. He would not answer that.

Meanwhile they began the short walk back to the camp-fire, Garrety a little ahead and sauntering. Suddenly he stopped and turned.

'Where's the shovel?' he said.

He stood shaking his head in a gesture of exasperation and looked away towards the camp, taking it for granted, Langhurst understood, that the shovel was his responsibility, though there had been no agreement on it, and that he was the one who should double back and get it.

He hesitated a moment. But something in him had shifted.

The weight he had felt was gone. The freshness and sweet air as the sun came up more strongly and birds chattered and shrilled, the easiness, among the surrounding trunks, with which his body fitted around him made contention for the moment a tedious and unnecessary thing. 'Dammit,' he said, but set off.

The shovel lay across a pile of dirt to one side of the hole. It looked out of place in the quietness, the remoteness of the clearing. He reached down and retrieved it, and when he stood again was struck, though his lightness of spirit did not desert him, by a strangeness, now that he was alone with the shivering of the leaves, a sense of spaces, beyond the trees, that he could not see into, opening into further spaces that even his mind might not reach; but he was not disturbed, did not feel in any way oppressed or threatened.

He looked at the hole they had dug. It did not change anything. Neither did the fact that he was here observing it. It made no gap in the stillness.

It was as if he and Garrety had never expended all that effort and sweat in digging it. They had only imagined that. Or so he might have believed if it wasn't for the weight of the shovel in his hand. Or if they had, the earth over long seasons had already covered it, and what it had been dug to contain.

The feeling was strange but not scary and made no difference to his mood or his consciousness of his own breath coming and going here among the breathing trees, or of the minute movement of leaves and of bark against bark, or a scurrying he was aware of, which must be bush mice or other unseen creatures, off in the brush. He heard Garrety striding back through the trees. But could scarcely be bothered to disguise the feeling of pleasurable, almost joyful but indifferent power he felt in belonging so completely to the morning and to his own skin.

'It's all right,' he shouted, to ward Garrety off for a moment. 'I've got it.'

'I thought you'd bloody fallen into that hole,' Garrety said stepping out among the trunks, and it was as if a burst of violent air had come blowing and blustering. 'What are you doing?'

'I lost something,' he said, 'that's all,' and with a false grin he held up the lucky coin he carried, 'my silver penny.'

Adair stepped out into the early light. Fresh scents, sharp with the sap of unfamiliar vegetation, made the chill air especially invigorating where it struck his face and burned in his nostrils. He took a deep breath, expanding his lungs. His soul stretched – that is how he thought of it. Considering how little sleep he had had, and his confused dreams, he felt light-footed, clear-headed, abounding in health, aware with a new keenness as he looked about and stepped into it of the beauty of the scene.

Under the effect of moonlight, or perhaps it had only been because of his tiredness, it had struck him last night as bleak and denuded, wind-swept high plains country. Now it had a kind of grandeur. All its bunched foliage fluttered and blazed out with a sap whose stickiness he could feel without even having to reach out and touch it. Birds were chittering and peeping. Wrens. Little flocks of them dipped low over the ground, then wheeled, rose in bunches. They were intent on the serious business, he knew, of feeding, but it had the look of play. Under the paper-barks close to the creek, the horses, fresh and lively, were involved in a carnival of their own, singly or in pairs in fluid motion back and forth as they scented the new day and felt the renewal of energy it brought them. The light on their flanks dimmed and flared, their dark manes lifted. In the changing space between them as they joined, then broke, came the flash of water.

Behind Adair, Daniel Carney came out. He stood rubbing his eyes a moment in the unaccustomed light. The shirt he wore hung in tatters. As the cold air struck him he bunched his shoulders, hugged his arms to his body to hold in its warmth.

'Kersey,' Adair called across to the fire. 'Fetch us some tea.'

They stood together in the honeyed sunlight, the man still hugging himself, shivering.

'You'll be all right,' Adair told him, 'when you get something warm into you. Here,' he said, when Kersey arrived with the two pannikins.

Daniel Carney cupped the pannikin with his cracked hands to get a little of the heat, then raised it and sipped. As the hot liquid flowed into him, his shoulders, which he had been holding stiffly against the cold, relaxed, and they stood side by side drinking the scalding tea, like two men about to set out on a mission, and so eager to begin they had no time to sit. Kersey, long-jawed and slack as ever, hung about with his jacket open waiting for their cups.

For God's sake, Adair thought, do you begrudge the man another two minutes to get a bit of warmth into him?

The others, the two young ones, were hunched at the fire. They looked so unhappy you might have thought they were the ones who were about to be strung up.

Daniel Carney had raised his head and was looking to where water glinted between the trees.

'Could I ask you a favour, sir? It's the last.'

Adair shifted his head.

'Could I, like, splash a bit of water over me face an' that? Wash. I'd feel –'

Adair felt Kersey's eyes upon him. A touch of colour came to his cheek.

'If you'd like,' he said at last. 'If you make it quick. Here,' he told Kersey briskly, and passed him the pannikins, first his own, then Carney's. He and the prisoner began to walk down to where the horses were tethered in the line of trees, leaving Kersey staring.

'What's 'e doin'?' Langhurst asked softly when Kersey, the pannikins hooked from the fingers of one hand, came back to the fire.

'Gawd knows,' he told them. 'He's gonna let him wash. He wants t' wash! Gonna let 'im skip, if you ask me.'

'Y' reckon?'

''E's a mad bugger. I wouldn' put it past 'im.'

They watched a moment, then Langhurst got to his feet and lightly, as if tracking two fugitives and eager to remain unseen, made his way from trunk to trunk till he came to the line of she-oaks and scrub-pine where the horses were.

He had no idea what he would do if, as Kersey suggested, Adair let the fellow go. There was a part of him that hoped he would. In the tender state that had come upon him in the clearing, and in which he still moved, he was willing to raise the sentence of death on any man. Every man.

Daniel Carney had paused. The horses moved this way and that all round him. Where was Adair? Then things cleared. Carney was standing with his hand on the neck of the chestnut bay. She gentled at his touch.

'There,' he said softly. Adair was beside him.

He offered the mare his open hand and she nuzzled at his palm and tongued for salt.

The horse was nervous, its flanks shivered. It lifted its feet in the sandy earth. The other horses, bunched a little way off, began moving again. The bay was still. Carney began to whisper to her, laying his face close to hers.

'You're all right, darlin'. Dannell's here. You know me. There's a pretty.' He whispered a name as if it was secret between them.

'Is that what he called her?' Adair asked. 'Kismet?'

Daniel Carney smiled. 'That was the name 'e give 'er. Cut 'er out of a mob an' trained 'er himself. It was like watchin' two dancers. I thought sometimes – you know, that he might of been one himself in another life. He had that look to 'im. He was six feet six in his socks – '

'I know,' Adair said.

'Jesus,' Kersey whispered from where he was watching. 'He's gonna let 'im get away. What'd I tell you? I told you, didn't I? He's gonna let 'im grab the horse!'

'So where does that leave us?' Garrety asked.

'Buggered if I know. We'd hafta chase 'im.'

'Again?' Garrety said. He too set off for the line of trees where Langhurst stood supporting himself against the trunk of a she-oak, its shadowy green in shawl-like motion about him.

'Shh,' he hissed as the others came up behind him, first Garrety, then, a minute later, Kersey as well.

They watched in a tight clump as the two figures, Adair in his jacket, cap and boots, the barefoot prisoner, came to the edge of the bank and Adair stopped, and the prisoner went on, slowly sinking from sight.

'This is crazy,' Garrety said.

He and Langhurst went forward briskly and came up behind Adair, who was unperturbedly standing. He barely turned his head to acknowledge them.

The man had crossed the first of the creek's three channels and waded out into the second, which was running fast round his legs, darkening the bottoms of his trousers and leaping in little waves over stones.

It was grey-blue mountain water, clean and cold-looking. The man reached down, scooped up a double handful and splashed it over his head, shivering at the icy coldness of it, though there was sunlight on his shoulders and hair. Slowly, with what appeared a loving care for the heaviness of his own flesh, he began to wash from his body the grime, the caked mud, the dried blood of his wounds, which the water as he laved bore away, a brief stain on its surface, to wherever the lie of the land was taking it; into some larger stream that would spread wide at first, then slowing, die out as so many of the streams did in this country, into marshes, or hundreds of miles on, via one stream then another, find its way to the sea.

Meanwhile he stood, his feet firmly placed on pebbles, and sluiced the glittering water over his neck and shoulders; for no reason now but the small pleasure it gave him, the touch of something alive and unconstrained. And against the sunlit channels that cut the sandy bed beyond, with its occasional stunted shrubs and bushes, and the grey-green foliage of the farther bank, his largeness bulked and imposed itself, the knotted shoulders, the breast to which the tatters of his thin shirt clung like a second skin, its shocking whiteness, with the marks, blue-black and livid, there and on his loins of Langhurst's boots.

Birds dipped and swerved over the water. Leaves flew out, an odd one here and there catching the sun, flashing out as if it were made of some other, finer material than the rest.

Slowly the man turned and stood with lowered head, observing with a child's interest the paleness of his feet through the swirling water. Almost done with himself now. With the business of washing off the long accumulation of dirt and sweat and blood, with the heaviness of the flesh.

In the modest pleasure of standing clean in the sunlight. In touch with that live element that on all sides was at play about him. Leaping over the bones of his feet where for a moment they made this unlikely interruption to its course. Eddying round them, then immediately fusing the broken light of its strands and tumbling playfully on.

The others watched. Caught off-guard by this unexpected interlude, they felt imposed upon, reduced to mere onlookers, to standing by and waiting on *his* time while, with O'Dare's permission it seemed, this fellow took all the time he needed, all the time in the world it might be, to just stand there idly running water over himself.

Langhurst looked sideways to see what the others might be thinking. He did not begrudge the fellow this spinning out of a few more minutes in the sun – any man might do that, if he could get away with it. But he was shocked by the nakedness of the man's injuries, the terrible rainbow colours that bloomed on his flesh. As if he were the one out there who stood stripped and exposed.

The man bent down to douse his head, and when he jerked it up again, all shining, the hair plastered to his skull like an otter's, his skull had the fierce look of an animal's, round and closed on its fierceness, but his body, as he bent and dragged up handfuls of water and let it spill in strands over his shoulders and breast, was dazzling. The solemnity of these simple activities caught in Langhurst's throat, and again he looked aside to see how Garrety was taking it.

Garrety too, who stood supporting his weight with one hand against the trunk of a she-oak, seemed impressed. He looked up with lowered head as if there were something here he could not directly fix his gaze on.

And at last it was enough. The man simply stood, staring down at his clean feet through the running water. The last of the world's muck was off.

Langhurst saw what it was then. Acutely aware suddenly of his own body, unwashed and stinking inside the prickly vest, the trousers stiff with dirt, of the dirt-balls between his toes, the dirt under his nails and ingrained in the cracks in his hands, the sully and stink of his armpits and groin, he thought: When all this is over I will go down and do what he is doing. I'll strip right off and wash. He felt already the clean touch of water laving over him, cold but clean, taking the dirt off, and had an intense desire to begin all over again with the freshness and sanctity of things. Let him take his time. It won't hurt us to wait a little. It's early yet. But another part of himself was impatient. To stand naked down there with his head wet and the clean cold water pouring over him. In just a little while now, he told himself. Half an hour at most. Not spelling it out. Not saying: When this feller is in the hole back there that me and Garrety just dug for him. When we have piled the last shovelful on to him. Into his mouth, over his eyes. Seeing now what this long ritual of washing and standing clean in the sunlight might be for, and that it was not, from the man's point of view, even considering what was to come, entirely useless.

And Adair?

He too stood watching. Relaxed. Quietened. Subdued to the rhythm of the man's reaching down, time after time, to the water and letting handfuls of it gush then trickle over his neck.

It should finish here, he thought. This is the natural end.

In the man's intense absorption in his task, and his own in watching, was a quietness he had been reaching for, he felt, for the whole of his life, for so long that he could not have said when the yearning for it, amid so much fret and action, had first come to him. Years back, in another country. When he had had no notion – how could he? – of

200

who it was who would be standing here, in what as yet unimagined landscape, watching an action so simple that it was hardly an action at all –

The man looked up then. Their eyes met. The moment was broken. The man moved, lifted his foot from the water, set it down in the clinging grains of sand. Returned, Adair thought, to this other condition we are bound to. Both of us. All of us. The insufficient law.

Epilogue

IN THE AFTERLIGHT of a late summer evening two men sit over the remains of a meal while a dark young woman, whom the observant guest suspects of standing in a closer relationship to the other than might be suggested by the eyes, in both cases lowered – one to the crumb-strewn cloth, the other to her work of whisking crusty fragments into a tray with a silver-backed and crested brush – moves with just the faintest whiff of sweat and vanilla sugar from his left side to his right. He considers the engravings above the sideboard: Morland – a fine set, which is what he would expect of his host; horses, hounds at the stretch, a view of rounded hills dark-stitched with hedges.

The conscious avoidance on his friend's part of that formal politeness between master and servant that would otherwise, he knows, be his natural demeanour, must violate another, more private code. He returns to the Morlands. The sense, almost forgotten out here, of the world's being so heaped and freighted as to overbalance with its own abundance, then the golden collapse into smoky autumn. Only when the woman, who is coarse-featured but in her own way trim and dignified, has restored the damask to glazed perfection, set a decanter and port-glasses before them and unobtrusively shut the door, does the middle-aged man let his breath out and speak.

The guest is Adair, who is to sail next day on the *Hyperion*, one of the ships that ride at anchor in the Cove; his host, an ex-army surgeon and veteran of the Peninsular, James Saunders. Adair has come to take charge of a bundle of letters that Saunders, a recent acquaintance, wants delivered to his family and to one or two friends at home. The slight tension between the two men has to do with the fact that one is leaving and the other not. There is always here some little play upon a difference so decisive, though it is disguised in Saunders' case, as is common between professionals and men of the world, with heavy banter. Adair knows his friend to be a man of intelligence and where his work at the hospital is concerned of quiet seriousness. He is also genuinely good-natured. He wishes sometimes that they could drop their joking manner and speak freely, but understands that without the cover of a playful cynicism Saunders might be too choked with shyness to say anything at all.

The harbour is not visible from where they sit. But hanging secure in Adair's head, like a ship in a bottle, is a miniature of the *Hyperion*, its furled sails drenched with moonlight, a riding-light in the fore-rigging, all preparations made for tomorrow's sailing. The captain, a bearded Scot called McAlister, is sitting up late in his stateroom below decks, completing the last of his reports. Barefooted sailors on the foredeck are telling yarns; their rough laughter spills out and one of them hawks and spits over the rails into the steep dark. Where the ship rides gently at anchor, waters of a glossy smoothness swallow and then disgorge the moon, and with it a quadrant of the southern heavens where, Canopus presiding, the constellations roll through a sky he will exchange before long for the more familiar northern one, like a side of his soul that has been in recession here; not lost nor denied but out of sight for a time – and who can say that he might not have had to come all this way, and entered into some opposite dimension of himself, to know at last what it was?

Saunders is speaking:

'As we know, this is a place that is always in the grip of rumour, the wilder and more unlikely they are the more our locals are inclined to believe 'em. They need this place to be outlandish, to deliver up marvels. To approximate, I would say, to the literary taste of the age – that is, to the mysterious, the nightmarish, the Gothic. Nothing else perhaps will justify the tedium for some, the terror for others, of being dumped here. It's natural enough. What else is there to divert them? News from over there is dead and stinking by the time it turns up among us. After five or six months at sea all the life has gone out of it, the immediacy. Whatever there might have been in it to hang a doubt on has already – out of our ken, of course – been resolved. A man can hardly be expected to hold his breath for a whole six months. People are hungry for diversion. For news, for gossip. It needn't be true. All it has to do is satisfy their notion of what might be true, their need for some bit of unexpected event that has the shape of a decent story – preferably, like all good stories, an old one in a new form. So you see, my friend, you do not quite get away. You leave here this shadow of yourself – not your real self, that would not serve – but this other more romantic, more outrageous self that fits the *story* and grows as it is passed on. Whether you like it or not, you have become – '

'Not me,' Adair protests.

'Oh yes, with all the qualifications I have just made. Most definitely. You don't get off as easily as that. You have done a great thing, my dear fellow, you have made yourself immortal. So long as any of us are here, I mean, to keep the story up.'

'This – hero, as you appear to think of him, does not even have my name.'

'No, but that's the master-stroke, or so it seems to me. He bears the *real* version of your name. O'Dare! Could anything be more appropriate? More indicative – I am interested in this aspect of the thing – of how the popular mind makes what it wants of the facts, dives deep down under them to discover that spark of inner truth that will bring the thing alive as fable. Didn't you know that O'Dare was one of your names? The name of this other you that the story has knocked up? For all your stern dedication to duty, my dear fellow, which none of us doubts, you are really, deep down, of the devil's party – that is, an Irishman, after all. To your health, Mr O'Dare, folk hero!'

Adair drank in the same spirit in which his jocular friend had proposed this toast; but as the unlikely agent of an event that had never in fact occurred, he regarded his pallid reflection in the glass above Saunders' mantelpiece with discomfort and a growing impatience to be done with all this. Not just the business itself but the jokiness. It was a style whose edgy mixture of worldliness and dry self-mockery he had never quite taken to.

Saunders had been regaling him with the latest version of his own legend; though the fact was, he had already heard it a dozen times over in the last week, from his barber, the Boots at the inn down by the quay where he had put up, the tedious fellows, shipping-clerks and chandlers' assistants, who composed the *table d'hôte* where he took his evening meal; each time in a slightly different form as it suffered the slippage of a detail added here, a suggestion there, according to the narrator's flair for story-telling or capacity for bold magnification, his assessment of the hearer's credulity, especially if it was a new chum, and his own sense of what was not but ought to have been true. He was,

205

frankly, sick of it. It had exhausted, in his view, whatever value it might have possessed as a mild joke; the best of which was that none of the story-tellers, even with the echo of the name as clue, had recognized in the rather dry fellow before them, with the crooked mouth and razored jaw that even at midday was in shadow, the embodiment of Irish effrontery and daring and Machiavellian guile that figured in such a daredevil manner in what they had to tell.

'It has, you see,' Saunders went on, 'all the ingredients. It's extraordinary how – complete it is. And how quickly all the elements have come together. What a well it is, the folk mind, of ignorance, speculation, the most extravagant sort of dreaming! It is Ossian, it is Homer, it is – if you will allow me a moment's blasphemy – Genesis, the Five Books. Our minds individually may be quite tame and hidebound, but put them together, let them just dip a little, each one, into the great ocean of dream, and what comes out is tremendous. It is noble, terrible – '

'Not quite in this case, surely.'

'No, but the reverberations are. And just think of the way so many disparate things have come together! I've been hearing bits and pieces of this stuff for the past fourteen years, and now, by a kind of chemical explosion, alchemy, they have combined, and there it is, pure gold. All jokes aside – and I'm sorry, old fellow, that you should be so – ambiguously mixed up in it, but I find the thing extraordinary.'

Adair did not commit himself.

The story when he had first heard it astounded him, but not for the reasons Saunders suggested. Where had it sprung from? How had so many details of a thing only he knew, and had communicated to no one, got out of his head and become general currency, begun to make the rounds of barber-shops and shipping offices and barracks and the dinner-tables of the better class of merchants and gentleman farmers? – an event merely dreamed, when his moral faculties were for a moment in abeyance in the other-world of sleep, an act, to him impermissible, out of a freer and different life. The authorities' insistence on having Daniel Carney done away with in secret, a hundred miles from the nearest place of settlement, had rebounded. Rumour was loose and had fabricated out of mere talk a story that for months now would muddy truth and haunt the place with unconfoundable ghosts.

At the last moment Daniel Carney had been saved – that was the nub of it. The Irish officer who had been sent out to oversee the hanging had all along been in on the thing, but had played so skilfully his part of lawman and public official that even the prisoner had been deceived. Some sort of unmasking had taken place during the night they had spent locked up together. At dawn the prisoner, still shackled, had hobbled down to the shores of a large lake, or inland sea. His chains were removed and he was allowed to wash. While the other troopers watched from a distance, a boat paddled by natives appeared, who were involved it seemed in the ordinary business of spearing fish. But suddenly the natives produced muskets, and under their covering fire, the officer and the convict both had clambered into the boat and been whisked away into the mist, the natives being in reality members of a settlement of disaffected ticket-of-leave men and runaway convicts who, over the nearly forty years of the colony's existence, had created, on the shores of a freshwater sea teeming with every sort of wildlife, a rival colony, a shadow Sydney as large almost as the original. Anyway, the officer, whose name was O'Dare, had become the hero of the hour, a true embodiment of the spirit of Irish resourcefulness and derring-do, and Daniel Carney a martyr miraculously resurrected; or O'Dare was a hateful renegade and confounder of the rule of law and Carney a dangerous rebel, once more on the loose.

Intelligent opinion in the colony had at first laughed at so much superstition and lurid fantasy.

There was no such thing, anywhere on the continent, as a golden city of escapees, an antipodean Cockayne run by riff-raff and runaway lords of misrule. And though the authorities had good hopes of discovering, somewhere in the interior, the long-promised and hoped for inland sea, there was no possibility from the scientific point of view of its being within a thousand miles of Curlow Creek.

But the powers, in offering this reasonable reassurance, made no headway against the thunderous combination of ignorance and seditious fervour on the part of the refractory Irish and panic in those good citizens for whom the notion of a shadow colony, a second Sydney in the hands of drunken felons, former cut-throats or thieves, was the stuff of nightmare, and the more easily believed because as everyone knew, and even the Governor had to admit, no man had ever been there to put rumour to the test.

'Which is what they will have to do, of course,' Saunders stated with assurance. 'Go out, I mean. And the sooner the better. It's no bad thing that all this should have forced our hand. An expedition. Ostensibly to explore the little problem of our river-system, which refuses, like so much else in the place, to conform to the rules. But also to scotch once and for all the rumours of that other settlement. And if along the way they should happen to stumble upon an inland sea – personally I have little hope of it, the inland sea is in my opinion a mirage! – all well and good. They will certainly find *something*. There's a lot of country out there.'

'There is,' said Adair, who had seen it.

'You have no further thoughts then?' Saunders asked when Adair had no more to add.

'On what?'

'Rival settlement, inland sea.'

Adair finished his port, set the glass down and gave the opinion that he had already delivered elsewhere.

'The last is possible,' he said, and lowered his gaze as there rose up and extended in his head that vast sheet of dazzling light he had come to the margin of in his dream, and his heart stirred a moment at the memory of its fish and birds, its promise of plenty. 'There is a puzzle, certainly, that we have not solved. The rivers must flow somewhere. But the first I would have thought mere cloud stuff – a bubble, a hoax.'

'Ah,' said Saunders lightly, 'and this from the man himself, the horse's mouth!' He sipped his port. 'And you are not tempted to be one of those to make the test? Who will go and find out?'

'You have heard some rumour to that effect?'

'Ah, rumours! I have heard they offered you the opportunity to take out a party – horses, oxen, collapsible boats –'

'To be the layer of my own ghost.'

Saunders laughed. He leaned forward to refill Adair's glass. Adair placed his hand across it. 'Yes,' he said. 'I too took it at first for a kind of joke.'

'But they did offer.'

'They did, yes.'

'And you –'

'Refused. It seemed,' he said, pausing to find the right word, 'unnecessary to add anything more than I have to the fascinating history of the place. I've done my bit, made my – contribution.' When Saunders laughed he saw that his reflection in the glass over the mantelpiece had permitted itself a dour smile. 'Even if it was an involuntary one, mere fantasy, and made under a false name. The fact is,' he said after a moment, 'I am tired of all this. It has cost me something. You may laugh – I do myself – at the absurdities that have come of it, but the thing itself – '

He did not go on. The rest of what he might have said dived underground, like one of those elusive rivers they had been speaking of, and Saunders, one eyebrow raised like a hook, was left hanging. He had no wish to speak of Daniel Carney, still less of Fergus; to add to speculation and mystery by admitting he had had his own purpose in being at Curlow Creek, and how much of himself he had left there – of his real self, of Adair – no less deeply buried than they were under a night, with its secrets and veiled desires, that was not the opposite of day but, for those who had entered its rich depths, the simultaneous underside of day, the swarming underside of life as it is lived, and as he would live it again, up there on the other side of the globe.

Later, a little light-headed from the wine he had drunk and still touched by the mood of what had been left unsaid, Adair made his way downhill towards the quay.

It may have been simply a tendency in himself, but it seemed to him that everything here, the lie of the land, the orientation and slope of the narrow streets, led in that direction: to the inns and dark little chandlers' shops along the shore that served the sea-life of the town, to the water-steps from which lighters set out with gear and provisions for the ships at anchor between the scrubby islands, or with rival shouts and offers, to tout for business with the new arrivals from Europe and the Indies; towards the great spread of water that opened, through rocky heads, to the Pacific and home. He meant to go down once more and

210

take a look at the *Hyperion*. He could scarcely contain his impatience now for dawn to come and their sailing-time. To be done at last with these years of moving from one place to another. To settle. To be at home.

To settle.

All round him here are the signs of a determination to confirm in this place a kind of permanency; which is not contradicted – quite the opposite – by so much that is unfinished. Even the grim bulk of the convict barracks when he comes to it – with its clock keeping local time, so many hours east of Greenwich, and behind it, slung in rows of hammocks, men sleeping out, as well as they are able, what each night contributes to their seven or fourteen years – has a new pile of rubble at its gates, where extensions are being made. It is hopeful, it is forward-looking. Even Saunders, for all his scepticism, would endorse that. But what it reaffirms in Adair just at this moment is his sense of displacement, a fear that what might be deepest in men is not this passion for making and building, for drawing the world within the confines of an established order, but some darker wish to annihilate the self with distance; that what we are really committed to in our hearts is unceasing motion, and what we raise in sunlight with the right hand, the left, out of a secret horror of the settled and stationary, will tear down in the dark.

'And is it really,' he asks himself, 'the settled life that I hope for? Is that why I am going home?'

He has written to Mama Aimée but not to Virgilia. It is not simply that any letter he might write now would have to travel on the ship with him, but that he wants at last to appear before her untrammelled and without intermediaries, in his own form, as himself; the new self that something in this harsh land and the events of these last months have created: a self that has journeyed into the underworld and come back both more surely itself and changed. He has discharged all she had asked of him as her agent in the search for Fergus, and if found, her emissary to him, and all that Fergus and his own conscience could demand in the way of brotherly affection and love. He is free. There is, at last, just the two of them. Free both, and with their lives before them. He will come to her in the assurance of what he has once and for all to offer, and which she must either accept or reject.

But now, with the light of a new day making pale the sky towards the ocean, the tide rising, a journey to begin, he cannot resist the vigorous swing of his own soul upwards out of the dark. There is a lightness in his blood that is not simply the last heady effects of the wine he has drunk but something essential: an optimism that never quite leaves him, that has never left him, for all the darkness he is capable of – an aspect, perhaps, of that sturdy good health Virgilia once teased him with – the body, the body – which keeps him rooted in life, committed to unending returns. But she had been speaking of herself as well. They are for life, both of them.

He is attracted as he walks on by an outpouring of light, unusual at this hour, from an open window a little below ground. When he approaches and leans down to see what it is, a rush of fierce heat strikes his face and through the flimsy stuff of his shirt.

It is a bakery. A lean fellow in loose trousers and a white cotton hat is pushing mounds of dough, that sit very plump and round on a long-handled shovel, into the mouth of an oven. Drops of sweat fly from his face. Pausing a moment to draw the back of his hand across his brow, he deposits another shovel-load deep into the oven's mouth. Adair watches entranced. A smell of yeasty dough, dark and intimate as seed, comes to him, with the sweeter one of baked crust.

An assistant, a pale youth of maybe sixteen, whose eyes and mouth are mere holes in a clown's face of powdered white, is punching with big fists and stringy, flour-dusted arms, at lumps of dough. He flips the dough and punches again. Baked loaves sit in rows on a tier of shelves.

They are baking the bread that before dawn will be delivered by horse-cart and boys with covered baskets through the streets of the town; to be sliced and dipped into steamy bowls of chocolate in the better houses and weighed out as rations in the convict barracks. Something in the ordinariness of this, the rough uniformity of the rows of loaves, but also in the orderly immemorial routine, this night work that keeps bakermen pale and fills the bellies of those whose business it is to break stones or tend sheep or stride about with their hands behind their backs making deals in the sun, pleases him. He stands watching, held by the swinging repetition of the men's movements.

'Hullo there,' he calls at last. 'Will you sell me a penny loaf?'

The clownface turns and squints to where he is leaning down out of the dark.

The man with the shovel makes a gesture and the boy takes one of the smaller loaves and hands it up to him. He pushes into his pocket for a coin.

'It's all right, sir, it's spoiled, as you see. Good luck to you.'

He raises his hand in thanks and walks on, holding his warm, spoiled loaf, the last gift of a place that has taken so much from him but has given him something too that he cannot measure yet, though more than he had expected.

He pauses a moment and pinches off a corner of the loaf,

the salty sweetness of the crust in his mouth a kind of blessing. He chews as he walks on, his saliva mixing with its sugars and driving new light into his heart, refreshing his mouth like common speech.